Stories of
the Pilgrims

Written by
Margaret B. Pumphrey

Revised and Edited by
Michael J. McHugh

Preface

The story of the Pilgrims has delighted youngsters for several generations. It is the inspiring story of how God raised up a tiny band of faithful Christians to establish Biblical Christianity in the New World.

This story helps children to see that faith in God enabled common people like the Pilgrims to triumph over persecution, hunger, and numerous hardships. Children also gain a great deal of knowledge regarding how youngsters lived during the early and mid 1600's.

Far too many young people in America today are being sheltered from the truth that our nation was originally founded upon the rock of Christian faith. It is the hope of the publisher that this reading text will, in some small way, help to provide the children of America with an understanding of our nation's rich Christian heritage.

May the good Lord bless all those who read this book.

Michael J. McHugh
Arlington Heights, Illinois

· A PUBLICATION OF ·

Christian Liberty Press

502 West Euclid Avenue, Arlington Heights, Illinois 60004

Table of Contents

Part I

From Old Homes to New

Table of Contents

Part II

Little Pilgrims and the Indians

Stories of the Pilgrims

Part I

From Old Homes to New

This was a busy day at Scrooby Inn

At Scrooby Inn

In the little village of Scrooby in England, three hundred years ago, stood a beautiful old house. It was the largest one in the village, and its moss-covered roof and large red chimneys rose high above the cottages around it.

The house stood close to the street, but behind it was a large garden where many bright flowers bloomed, and a row of tall trees cast their pleasant shade. On one side of the garden were three round ponds. For a hundred years these ponds had never failed to supply fish for the Friday dinner.

A great rosebush clung to the walls of the house. For years it had climbed and climbed, until now some of its clustering red blossoms peeped into one of the upper windows. The whole room was sweet with their fragrance. This old house had once been a fine palace, but now it was used as an inn where travelers might stay for the night.

In the stables beyond the garden there were some horses that belonged to the king. When his messengers carried his letters to the North Country, they always stopped here to change horses and rest for an hour.

Only a few miles from Scrooby was a famous old forest. Every child in the village knew the story of Robin Hood and his merry men who had once lived in this forest. They often played "Robin Hood;" it was the game they liked best of all.

Once a party of the king's friends, who were going to the forest to hunt, had stayed all night at the inn. This was a time always remembered by the children who lived at Scrooby Inn. They seemed never to tire of talking about the packs of hounds, the beautiful horses, and the riders in their colorful hunting dress. Then there was the dinner in the great dining hall, and best of all, the long evening when they all sat around the fireplace and listened to the stories the hunters told.

The landlord, William Brewster, had not been pleased to have his children hear so much about life at the king's court, so they had been sent to bed much earlier than they wished. The next morning when they awoke, the noisy hunting party had gone. Had they really been there at all? Was it not all a bright dream?

One June morning Jonathan Brewster brought into the garden the new boat he had just finished. He was going to sail it upon the fish pond. His little sisters, Fear and Patience, stood near watching the tiny boat make its first trip across the pond. Fear held in her arms a small wooden doll, very ugly, but very dear to the little mother. Jonathan wanted the doll for a passenger, but Fear would not put her baby in the boat until she was sure it would not tip over.

The little ship had hardly touched the other side when a distant sound made the children spring to their feet and listen. Again they heard the long, clear sound of the bugle.

"It is the king's messenger! Run and tell Henry to get out a fresh horse!" cried Patience. But Jonathan was already far down the path, calling the stable boy as he ran.

Patience drew the forgotten ship out of the water and ran into the house to tell her father.

There was a high, stone wall around the house and garden, and, just outside the wall, a ditch filled with water. The bridge over the ditch might be drawn up so none could cross, but this was not often done.

When Master Brewster came out to unlock the great iron gate, Patience and little Fear were close at his side. They always felt afraid of the tall messenger who looked so stern and said so little, but they loved to hear the clatter of swift hoofs, and to see horse and rider dash through the gate into the yard.

They had not long to wait. Again the sound of the bugle was heard, very near this time. Another minute, and into the village street galloped the beautiful black horse bearing the king's messenger.

The stable boy ran to meet him at the gate and held the horse's head while the man sprang to the ground.

"I have a message for you, Master Brewster," he said. "Queen Anne, with her knights and ladies, journeys from her home in the North. They will rest for the night in your house."

Patience waited to hear no more, but flew into the house to tell her mother this wonderful news.

"Mother! Oh, Mother!" she called. "Where is Mother?"

From room to room she ran until she found her quiet, sweetfaced mother at her spinning wheel.

"Oh, mother, the queen is coming here to stay all night! She has ever so many knights, and ladies, and servants with her. May I help get the best bedroom ready for the queen? The messenger has come, and he is telling father all about it."

"What are you talking about? You are excited, Patience."

"The child is right," said her father, who had just come into the room. The queen is on her way to her new home in England, you know, and the party will spend the night here."

"There is little time to prepare for royal guests, but we will make them welcome," said Mistress Brewster, quietly.

Comprehension Questions

1. What had this beautiful old house been before it was used as an inn for travelers?

2. Why were some of the king's horses kept in the stables?

3. What did the children enjoy most of all about the hunting parties stopping in at the inn?

"She looked down at the children and smiled"

A Royal Guest

This was a busy day at Scrooby Inn. Before the sun had set, the large house with its fifty rooms had been made ready to receive the party. The long table in the dining hall was spread with the finest linen. In the kitchen the three big brick ovens were filled with browning bread, cakes, and other dainties. Fowls were being roasted before the open fire.

Many times that afternoon the children ran to an upper window to look for the royal guests. The sun sank lower and lower, but still they did not come.

"Perhaps they have lost their way," said Fear.

"They will have a guide, so they cannot lose their way," replied Jonathan, "but perhaps they have been met by robbers."

In those days travelers were often overtaken by bands of rough men who robbed them of money and horses. So Jonathan's words filled their hearts with dismay. There were three very sober little faces in the window.

But before the sun was quite gone, the thrilling note of a bugle was heard and those faces brightened in a moment. Out of a little grove far down the road, appeared a company of horsemen. Nearer and nearer they came until the first rider, proudly bearing the red and gold banner of his queen, was in plain view.

Upon the shining spears and plumed helmets of the knights who rode behind him, fell the last rays of the setting sun, making them glisten like gold.

Within the square formed by the horsemen was a splendid coach, heavily carved and richly gilded. Upon the driver's seat rode two coachmen dressed in colorful clothing of red and gray. Two footmen sat upon the high seat behind. The coach was drawn by six fine black horses, which arched their beautiful necks and daintily lifted their slender feet as they sped toward the village.

The party was soon so near that the sound of the horses' feet could be heard, and sometimes, the clear ring of their silver bridles.

The news of the royal visit had spread through the town, and at every gate was a group of villagers eager to greet the queen and her party. As they rode through the street the air rang with cries of, "Long live the queen!"

The great gates of Scrooby Inn were thrown open, and a maid was sent to bring the children into the garden, where William Brewster and his entire household had gathered to receive the queen.

There was a moment of breathless waiting, then over the bridge and into the yard swept the dazzling company of knights, and the splendid coach.

The footmen sprang to the ground and opened the doors. Again rang the cry, "Long live the queen!"

Jonathan waved and shouted with the rest, but little Patience was silent. As she glanced from one to another of the four ladies who stepped from the coach, a look of disappointment clouded her face. She was looking for a lady with many strings of jewels around her bare throat, and a sparkling crown upon her head.

Patience had seen pictures of many queens; all had worn crowns and jewels. Surely there was no queen in this party. "Jonathan, where is the queen? I do not see her," she whispered, tears of disappointment filling her eyes. "Hush!" answered Jonathan, softly. "That is she in the blue velvet gown and the hat with the long white plumes. You did not think she would wear a crown when traveling, did you?"

Perhaps the lady may have heard something for she looked down at the children and smiled. As Patience looked into the kind, beautiful face, her disappointment melted away and she forgave the queen for not wearing her jewels.

Jonathan and Patience and Fear saw very little of the queen and her company that night, for Mistress Brewster believed that children should be neither seen nor heard when there were strangers at the inn.

It seemed very hard to go to bed at the usual time when there were knights and a real queen in the house. They were sure they could not go to sleep; but when Mistress Brewster went to their beds half an hour later, all three were in a dream land of kings and queens, knights and ladies, castles and deep forests.

Patience wakened very early the next morning. She dressed quickly and went down to the garden to gather fresh flowers for the breakfast table. Yet, early as she was, some one was there before her. A lady was bending over a bush of beautiful roses; when she turned, Patience saw it was the queen.

The child bowed in the quaint, pretty way her mother had taught her. She was wondering whether she ought to go back into the house, when the lady smiled and said:

"I am admiring your roses. How fresh and pretty they are with the dew still on them!"

"This bush is my very own," said Patience, as she gathered some blossoms for the lady. "I call these the Bradford roses because William Bradford gave the bush to me."

"And who is William Bradford?"

"Oh, he is a young friend of Father's. He does not live in Scrooby, but he comes here to church every Sunday, and so do Master Chilton and his family and ever so many others. We have a large chapel in our house right over the dining room. Nearly everyone in Scrooby comes here to church, and some people come as far as twenty miles."

"I noticed a beautiful church as we rode through the village yesterday," the lady said. "I should think you would all go there."

"That is King James's church," answered Patience. "If we go there we have to worship just as he wishes us to.

Father thinks the king's way is not right. Almost every one around here says the king's way is not right, so we do not go to his church."

"King James would not like to hear that," said the queen, gently, "and it would not be safe for you to talk to every stranger so freely."

Poor little Patience! What had she said! Suddenly she remembered that she had been telling a very great secret. Her face turned as red as the roses and her eyes filled with tears.

"Never mind, little one," said the queen, kindly. "Your secret is safe with me. Let us forget all about it."

Then she talked to the child about the flowers, and Patience took her to see the lilies that grew in one of the ponds in the garden.

An hour later three children stood at the gate of Scrooby Inn, watching a gilded coach and a company of horsemen disappear down the road.

Soon the coach was gone and the last glistening spear was lost to sight. Although she never saw her again, Patience always remembered the beautiful queen who shared her secret.

Meeting in Secret

For a time all went well, but after a few months King James was told that the people of Scrooby were not going to Scrooby church. Everybody knew they were men and women who worshiped God, so they must have meetings somewhere.

One Sabbath morning two strangers came to Scrooby. As they walked through the street they noticed a number of people going into William Brewster's house.

"I believe they are going there to worship," said one of the men.

"I think so, too, but we will wait until we are sure," answered the other.

Far down the road they saw a carriage coming, so they stepped behind a wall. The carriage came slowly on and turned in at Brewster's gate. In it were John Robinson and his family. The men knew this man was a pastor from the way he was dressed, and so knew that they had found the place where the people were at worship.

A little later they went into the house and up the stairs. There in the chapel they found John Robinson preaching to his people.

The strangers handed him a message from the king and left the room.

After Master Robinson had finished speaking he read the message. Even the little children felt that this letter meant trouble for those who had come there to worship God.

"My friends," said their pastor, "King James has ordered us to go to his church and worship according to the laws of England, or not worship at all. He says if we do not obey him we shall be punished."

What could the good men and women do? They did not believe as the king did, and thought it was not right for them to go to his church. They would not do what they believed to be wrong.

For several minutes all were silent. Then William Bradford spoke.

"This house will be watched every Sabbath," he said. "This large, pleasant room has been our church home for a long time, but it will not be safe to meet here any more."

After talking for a while about the best thing to be done, the pastor prayed that God would help and protect them, and all went sadly home.

After some time King James heard that the people were not yet going to the village church, and again he sent his men to Scrooby.

"Watch William Brewster's house and take every man who goes there on Sunday," he said.

The next Sunday two soldiers watched that house. They watched the front door and the back door, but not a person did they see. Had the people obeyed the king and gone to the old church? No, indeed! The soldiers were watching the wrong house. If they had been at the other end of the village they might have seen where the people went to worship that morning.

The next Sunday the worshipers met at Doctor Fuller's and the week after that at Master Allerton's. Each Sabbath they met in a different house, and each Sabbath the soldiers tried to find them. At last they met only at night, when it was harder for the soldiers to see where they went.

William Brewster was an elder in John Robinson's church. The pastor did not live in Scrooby, and sometimes he was not able to go to meeting. Then Elder Brewster led the service.

One very dark winter night they again met at Elder Brewster's house. The last persons to come were Master Chilton and his little daughter, Mary. Her face was pale, and her hands trembled as she tried to untie her hood.

"What is the matter, Mary?" asked Mistress Brewster, helping her to take off her wraps. "Are you so cold?"

"I have had such a fright!" said the child. "There are two soldiers at your gate, Mistress Brewster. Father and I did not see them until we were almost at the bridge. We did not look toward the house but walked right by, as though we were not coming here. When we were sure they were not following us, we went around and came in by the stable gate."

Elder Brewster looked out of the window. Yes, there were two men walking up and down in front of the house.

"Brewster's house is dark and still. There is no one there," said one. "They are obeying the king very well."

"No doubt they are all asleep, as we ought to be. I am stiff with cold," answered the other as they walked away. They would have been much surprised if they had seen the little group on their knees in the dark chapel upstairs.

When the meeting was over they did not all go home at once. The soldiers would notice so many people together and know they had been to some place to worship.

Still King James did not believe the people were obeying him. He thought if these soldiers could not find where the meetings were held, he would send some who could.

Comprehension Questions

1. What did two strangers notice about the Brewster's house?

2. What did the message from the king say?

3. Did the people go back to the Scrooby church or did they continue to meet with each other?

4. Why did the king's soldiers have trouble finding where the people were meeting?

5. What was happening in the Brewsters' house when the soldiers saw that it was dark?

For Conscience' Sake

Up in the loft of a large barn, John Robinson was teaching his people. He held his Bible in his hand, but he could not see to read it, for only the pale moon lighted the loft. They knew many chapters of the Bible, however, and repeated one softly.

Suddenly they heard voices outside. "I saw two men go into this barn," said one soldier.

"And I saw a woman and two children," said another. "I believe they are meeting for worship. Let us find out. Come, men."

Up in the loft the people heard and trembled. The men tried to hide the women and children in safe places, then turned to face the soldiers.

Up the old stairs they came. "We have found you at last," they cried. "Come with us."

So the men were taken away to prison and their families returned to their lonely homes. After a few weeks the prisoners were set free; but still they would not attend the king's church.

Many times they were put in prison, and some of their homes were burned. They were very, very unhappy.

One day the men of the little church met to talk about their troubles and plan some way to help matters.

"It will never be safe to worship God as the Bible requires around here. Even now three of our friends are in prison, and the rest of us may be there by night," said one.

"I fear we must leave England," said their pastor, "yet I do not know where we could go to be free. We should be in just as great danger in many other countries."

"You know I spent several years in Holland, when I was a young man," said Elder Brewster. "There every one is free to worship as he likes, and so many people come from France, England, and Spain. The Dutch are glad to have honest people from any land make homes in their country."

Then he told them about the fine godly schools in Holland, where they could send their children; and about the fishing fleets, the beautiful cities, and the great silk and woolen mills where they could all find work.

Holland was not very far from England, so it would not cost as much to go there as to some other places. After thinking about it for some time, it was decided that all who could would go to Holland in the autumn.

All summer they quietly planned how to leave England. They dared not speak of it openly for fear the king's men might hear and put them in prison again. King James was not willing to permit them to find homes in another country. When autumn came, the crops had been gathered and sold. The men had sold their horses and cattle, their homes and nearly all of their furniture. Their clothing and a few other things were packed in boxes, and at last they were ready to start on their journey.

It made them very sad to leave England. They loved their country. They loved their green fields and pleasant village and the homes where they had once been so happy.

"We are Pilgrims now," they said, "and we will wander on until we find a home where we can serve and worship God freely."

Comprehension Questions

1. When the soldiers found the people worshiping in a barn, what did they do to the men?

2. What happened to some of their homes?

3. What did the men decide they must do to be free to worship God according to the Bible?

4. List three of the reasons Holland was thought to be a good country in which to move.

5. At what time of the year did the people sadly leave England?

*"On a wooden box sat a mother with her baby
asleep in her arms"*

Pilgrims

The next night the stars looked down upon a strange sight. On the shore of the sea near a large city, a group of Pilgrims waited for the ship which was to carry them to Holland.

It grew very late. One by one the lights of the city went out, and all was dark and still. Even the little waves seemed to speak in whispers as they crept up to the shore.

On a wooden box sat a mother with her baby asleep in her arms. Two tired little children, with the cold sand for a bed and a blanket for a pillow, slept beside her. Some of the older children were too excited to sleep. They amused themselves by throwing pebbles into the water or playing in the sand.

Others of the company sat on boxes or on the sand, talking in low tones. They did not speak about the homes and friends they were leaving. That would make them too sad. They talked of better times they would have in their new homes.

One by one the children fell asleep, some on the cold sand, others pillowed in their mothers' arms.

As the night wore on the men paced anxiously up and down the shore. They peered out over the black water hoping to see the dark form of the vessel that was to take them to Holland. At any time the soldiers might be upon them. Every minute they waited on the shore added to their peril.

Watchmen were placed at points along the shore to warn the Pilgrims of any approaching danger.

A terrible dread was sinking into their hearts. What if the ship should not come at all? What if the soldiers should suddenly swoop down upon them? But these thoughts they would not speak aloud. They tried to cheer each other with encouraging words.

From a distant clock tower the bells chimed three. The Pilgrims drew closer together and spoke in hushed voices.

"Are you quite sure this is the place where the captain of the ship promised to meet us?" asked William Bradford.

"This is the very spot, just where this little brook flows into the sea," answered Elder Brewster.

"It will soon be dawn," said John Robinson. "I fear daylight will find us still waiting here for the ship."

"That must not be," replied Elder Brewster, "for the soldiers would soon be upon us. If the ship does not come within an hour we must seek the homes of our friends. Hark! What is that? I thought I heard the splash of oars."

In silence they listened, straining their ears to catch the sound. Again they heard it, and their hearts leaped with hope and thankfulness.

A moment later a boat rowed by two men was seen approaching the shore. Quickly and quietly the boat was loaded and rowed back to the ship, which lay out in the deep water. Then it returned for another load, and another, until all the people and their goods had been carried to the ship.

"Now, Captain, let us set sail at once, and by daylight we shall be safe out of the king's reach," said Elder Brewster.

"Oh, do not be too sure of that," said a stern voice by his side. In a moment the Pilgrims found themselves surrounded by soldiers.

"What does this mean, Captain?" cried Elder Brewster. But the captain was nowhere to be seen. He was ashamed of his wicked deed and dared not face the men whom he had betrayed into the hands of the soldiers.

It was of no use to resist the king's men, so when the first gray light of morning came, the Pilgrims again stood on the shore.

Last night the stars had twinkled merrily when they saw the Pilgrims about to escape King James. Now they saw them with their burdens on their backs, and their children in their arms, going toward the large, black prison. The little stars still twinkled faintly but seemed to say, "Be brave! The One who made us and made you is stronger than King James." Then one by one they closed their eyes, as if unwilling to see the prison doors close upon women and babies.

In a few days the doors of the prison opened again, and the women with their children passed out. I think they were not so very glad to be free, for their husbands were still in prison and they had no homes to which they might go. Some had friends there in the city who gladly welcomed them. Others returned to Scrooby where they lived with friends and neighbors. It was several months before all the men were allowed to return to their families.

Because he had hired the ship and made most of the plans for leaving England, Elder Brewster was the last to leave the prison. He soon found Mistress Brewster and the children in the old house which had always been their home. Another man kept the inn now, but he and his wife were kind-hearted people and had gladly opened their house to these homeless ones.

"Jonathan seems two years older than he did last fall," said his father that night, after the children had gone to bed.

"Yes, Jonathan is quite a man for his thirteen years. He helps care for the horses and does many errands for the innkeeper. The girls, too, help around the house, that they may not be a burden to these kind people."

"Tomorrow we will look for a little home of our own, where we can be comfortable until spring." said Elder Brewster.

"And what shall we do in the spring?" asked Mistress Brewster.

"Go to Holland!" answered her husband.

Comprehension Questions

1. How were the Pilgrims planning to get to Holland?

2. Why were they worried when the ship came so late?

3. Whom did they meet when they thought they were safely on the ship?

4. Where was everyone put when they were taken off the ship?

5. Why was Brewster the last man to be allowed to leave the prison?

Away to Holland

When spring came, the Pilgrims again planned to leave England. Elder Brewster knew a Hollander who had a ship of his own. So he arranged with this Dutch captain to carry the Pilgrims to Holland.

They now went to a lonely place on the shore far from any town where they thought they would be safer. All day they waited for the ship, fearing every minute to be taken by the king's men.

At last, late in the afternoon, a sail appeared. When the ship had come as close to the shore as it could, it anchored and waited for the people to row out to it. The Pilgrims had a large boat of their own in which they had brought their goods down the river to the sea.

It was agreed that most of the men should go first and load the heavy boxes upon the ship, then two come back for those left on shore. The boat had started toward the shore for its second load when the ship's captain saw something which filled his heart with terror. A long black line was curving down the hill. He raised his glass to his eyes. "Soldiers and horsemen! Look, men!" he cried.

One glance told them that the soldiers were marching straight toward the place where the Pilgrims were waiting.

"Quick! Lower another boat!" cried William Bradford. "We can row to the shore and get the others before the soldiers reach them."

But already the sailors were lifting the anchor. The wind filled the sails and the ship began to move.

"Let us off," cried the men. "If you are afraid to wait for the others, at least let us go back to our families."

"The soldiers will capture my ship," answered the captain. "My ship is all I have in the world. They shall not have it."

"They do not want your ship, and they could not reach it if they did. They only want us. Let us go!"

But the frightened man would not listen to them. He had heard of many captains who had lost their ships through helping people escape from England, and he would not stop a moment. The ship sailed out into the sea, and the darkness soon hid the shore from the sight of those on deck.

That night a great storm arose. The little ship was tossed about like a chip upon the waves. Not a star was to be seen in the black sky to guide the pilot. No friendly lighthouse sent out its rays to show them where to go.

For more than a week the ship was driven before the wind, they knew not where. When the storm was over, the sailors found they had been going away from Holland instead of toward it. They were hundreds of miles off of their course.

"If we have a good wind and fair weather we shall reach port in a few days," said the captain when the ship had been turned and headed for Holland.

But they did not have a good wind and fair weather. That very night a heavy fog settled down upon the sea. They could not see ten feet from the ship. Two days later another storm came up, much worse than the first one.

Surely the little vessel could not brave the storm. One of the masts was gone, and the water poured in though a hole in the side of the boat. Worst of all, the food and fresh water were almost gone. None on board expected ever to see land again.

The captain thought God was punishing him for his cowardly act in leaving the helpless women to the soldiers. The sailors all joined the Pilgrims in their prayers for help and pardon.

At last the clouds broke, and bits of blue sky peeped forth. Soon the wind went down, and the waves, too, slowly grew quiet. With the sun to guide them by day, and the stars by night, the ship finally reached the city of Amsterdam in Holland.

But what had become of the Pilgrims who had been left on the shore?

When the soldiers came up they found only a group of very miserable women, frightened children, and two or three men. They saw the ship sailing out to sea and knew they were too late to take those they most wanted.

What should they do? It seemed a shame to imprison women and children who had done no one any harm. But they had their orders, and there was nothing to do but obey.

So the Pilgrims were placed in their boat and rowed to the city. It was a long, tiring ride, and before they reached the landing the night had grown quite dark, and most of the children were fast asleep.

When the lights of the city were seen, one big soldier thought of his wife and babies there, safe at home. Then he looked at his prisoners, a few tearful women and some tired, sleeping children. He did not feel very brave. Risking his life in battle was more pleasant than this.

The other soldiers seemed to feel much as he did, for when the shore was reached, they gently helped their prisoners from the boat. Then each took a sleeping child in his arms and soon all disappeared down the dark street.

The Pilgrims were not kept in prison long this time. A few days later they returned to the homes of their friends. The judges were tired of them. The king, too, was tired of the trouble.

"Since their husbands have gone, let the women go to them. I am tired of hearing about it," said King James.

But few of them had money to go then, and it was many months before the men in Holland could earn enough money to send for their families.

Comprehension Questions

1. As the people were getting on another ship in the spring to go to Holland, what did the captain notice?

2. Why did the captain want to hurry away and not get the women and children who were left on the shore?

3. What did the captain think God was doing to him when they had terrible storms and were almost going to sink?

4. When the soldiers found the women and children what orders did they obey?

5. What did King James finally let the women do?

"From this high road the Pilgrims . . . could see beautiful churches, large shops, and narrow streets"

In Holland

At last the ship bearing the rest of the Pilgrims reached Holland. The captain had told them that soon they would land in Amsterdam. All were upon the deck eager to catch the first glimpse of the city which was to be their home.

"If it were not for this fog, I think you could see the city now," said one of the sailors to the group of children at the bow.

They peered into the mist, but not a sign of the city could they see. Above, a ball of soft, yellow light showed where the sun was trying to shine through the haze. Sometimes a great, shadowy sail floated toward them out of the mist. Many little fishing boats passed quite close to the ship.

In one of these a little boy sat on the big brown net piled up in one end of the boat. He looked up and saw the children on the ship high above him, and waved his hand. Of course, the children waved to him, and of course, when their ship had passed the little fishing boat, they ran to the other end of the deck and waved again. They waved until boy, net, and boat were all lost in the fog.

Then the children turned again to watch for the city. "Oh! Oh!" cried Jonathan Brewster.

"O-o-o-o-oh!" echoed a dozen others.

What was it they saw? Out of the mist rose high, shining towers, golden church spires, and tall pointed roofs with wonderful chimneys. For a minute all were speechless.

"The city looks as though it were floating right on the water," said Mary Chilton, when she had found her voice.

"It is, almost," answered her mother. "I am told there is water all around it, and through it. In many of the streets are waterways where boats pass to and fro between the houses."

"How beautiful it is!" said Mistress Brewster, who had just come up onto the deck with baby Love in her arms. "I am sure we shall be very happy here. See, the sun is coming out and the mist is almost gone."

It took the ship a long time to make its way past the other boats in the harbor, and up to the landing. On the shore stood a number of Englishmen who had waited hours for this ship to arrive. Some had lived in Holland several years, but most of them were Pilgrims who had been carried away from England in the Dutch ship.

Mary Chilton's eyes moved quickly from one to another of the men on the shore. She was looking for a beloved face. "There he is, there!" she cried. "Mother, Mother, there is Father! He does not see us. Wave your handkerchief!"

The Brewster children had soon picked out their young friend William Bradford, and were waving and calling to him, though the deep shouts of the sailors drowned their voices. Nearly everyone had seen some dear friend in the group on the shore.

Would the ship never make the landing? How very slow the sailors were!

Most of the men had prepared little homes for their families. They had rented small houses near together, that they might not be lonely in the strange city.

"I have taken a cottage for you near Master Robinson's," said Bradford to Elder Brewster when greetings were over. "It is not such a fine large house as your home in Scrooby, but it is comfortable."

"You are very kind," answered the older man. "We do not need a large house. If it will shelter you and us, it is large enough." "Yes," said Mistress Brewster, "we want you to make our house your home until you have one of your own."

Bradford thanked his friends, then, taking little Fear in his strong arms, he led the way.

Before them was what looked to be a long hill, very flat on top. There were stairs up the side and when these had been climbed, the Pilgrims found themselves on a wide, smooth road. They were as high as the tree tops and could look down upon the shining red roofs of the houses.

On many of the chimneys were great nests of sticks and straw. In some of them the Pilgrims saw young storks with their hungry mouths wide open for the frogs or little fishes their mothers brought them. On one chimney the mother bird sat on the nest and the father stood on one leg beside her, guarding his home. He must have known there was no danger, for he seemed to be fast asleep.

From this high road the Pilgrims looked over the cottages into the pretty gardens behind them. They could see beautiful churches, large shops, and narrow streets.

In every direction they saw great windmills with four long arms stretched out to catch the breeze. They were taller than the highest houses, and one might fancy them to be giant watchmen guarding the city.

Beyond the town were a river and a large lake and in the city itself were scores of little streams running in every direction. How strange it looked to see hundreds of masts and sails scattered about among the trees and houses!

On the other side of the road was the sea with the shining sails of many ships. How broad and smooth the water looked!

"Is this a hill, or did the people build this high street?" asked one of the boys.

"This is a dike," answered Bradford. "Holland is a very low country. In many places it is lower than the sea, so the people have built these strong walls of earth and stone to keep the water from overflowing the land."

"When the hard storms come, will they not push the dike over?" asked Patience.

"No, they cannot do that, because the wall is so much wider at the bottom than at the top; but the waves often dash high against the dike. They seem to try to get through the wall. The wind helps them, but the dike is too strong.

"Yet sometimes the water does make its way through the wall. At first only a tiny stream of water is seen trickling down the side of the dike. If this leak were not mended at once, the stream would soon grow larger and larger until nothing could stop it. The land would be flooded and many people lost.

"Every day and every night watchmen go up and down looking for a leak in the wall. When they find one, they ring a large bell, and all who hear it run to the dike to help stop the leak. They know there is not a moment to be lost if they would save their homes. Their swift fingers weave mats of straw which they crowd into the hole. Then, with earth and stone, the wall is made as strong as before. Even the little children are taught to watch for a leak in the dike."

Then he told them how a whole city was once saved by one brave little Hollander who held back the water by filling a tiny leak with his small hand.

Comprehension Questions

1. Why was it difficult to see the city of Amsterdam as they came close to it?

2. What did they think about the city when they could see it?

3. Do you remember why many of the fathers were already in Holland?

4. What was the high hill that helped the Pilgrims to look over the city?

5. What is the purpose of a dike?

The Home in Amsterdam

The Pilgrims soon found the street where their new homes were. But how different it was from the streets of Scrooby!

Down the middle of it was a broad stream of water called a canal. On each side of the canal was a narrow road paved with stones. The roads were not wide enough for a horse and wagon. When the people wished to ride, or had heavy loads to carry, they used a boat on the canal.

The houses looked more odd than the streets. They were made of brick of every shade of red and pink, and yellow. They stood close to the street and quite near together. But strangest of all, many of them did not stand straight.

This is because they were not built upon walls of stone, as ours are. These houses were built upon long posts driven deep into the earth. In Holland the ground is often soft and wet. The weight of the house often makes the posts sink in deeper on one side than the other, and then the house leans to one side.

When William Bradford reached the house he had taken for his friends, he unlocked the front door with a huge brass key. Then the Brewsters stepped into - the hall or the parlor do you suppose? No, they were in the kitchen, for that was the front room in a Dutch house. The sitting room looked out on the pretty garden behind the house.

"'Hodgepodge for our supper,'
said Bradford, peeping into the kettle"

But the kitchen was often the dining room and sitting room, too. At night it was very likely to be a bedroom as well, though you would never think it until you saw the strange box-like bed drawn from its hiding place in the wall.

In this kitchen the floor was made of tiles. There were fresh, white curtains in the little windows, and a row of blossoming plants on one of the window sills. A long shelf held a row of plates, a blue and white water pitcher and two tall candles.

There was the quaintest little fireplace in the room. It looked like a great brass pan filled with hot coals. A long chain from the shelf above it held a shining copper kettle. How it boiled, and bubbled making its bright little lid dance merrily!

"That is hodgepodge for our supper," said Bradford, peeping into the kettle.

"What is hodgepodge? I hope it tastes as good as it smells."

"Indeed it does, Jonathan. It is the best stew of meat and vegetables you ever tasted. Our neighbor, Mevrow van Zant, taught me how to make it. Here are some little seedcakes she gave me for you children. Our Dutch neighbors are very kind. They have done much to help us make the homes ready for our friends."

When bedtime came, Mistress Brewster took Fear and Patience upstairs to their own little room. In the corner was a large bed quite hidden behind long curtains which reached from ceiling to floor. When Patience pulled back the curtains and saw the high feather bed she thought she would need a little ladder to get into it.

Patience thought she would need a little ladder to get into this bed

As their mother tucked the children in and kissed them good night, Patience whispered, "Isn't this just like a dream! I fear when I waken in the morning this nice little house will be gone, the windmills and canals, the boats, the storks, and the dikes will all be gone, and we shall be in England again."

Comprehension Questions

1. How did the people of Holland travel or move heavy loads?

2. Why were many of the homes not standing straight?

3. What is hodgepodge?

4. How did the Dutch neighbors treat these new people from England?

5. What was Patience afraid of as she was tucked into bed?

On the Canal

The next morning, after the pretty blue and white dishes were washed, the kettles scoured, and fresh white sand sprinkled on the kitchen floor, Patience took baby Love and went out on the doorstep to watch the boats on the canal.

There were many of these boats passing to and fro. Some carried fuel or grain. Some carried fish, and others were loaded with boxes of goods from the mills. Some were passenger boats and carried people from one town to another.

Soon Jonathan came out with a large stone jar which he set upon the wall of the canal. On the next doorstep sat Mary and Remember Allerton, and they, too, had a large jar. There was one at Mistress Chilton's door, and all up and down the street might be seen these brown jars.

What were they for? Water, to be sure! These children were waiting for the water barge to come along and fill their jars. This seems strange in a land where there is more water than anything else. But the water in the canals is not fit to drink, so the people must buy fresh water every day. This is brought from the river far beyond the city.

While the children waited for the water barge, they saw a large boat coming down the canal. There was no wind, so the sail was down. At first they could not see what made it glide along so easily. As it came nearer they saw that there was a long rope tied to the bow, and the boat was being drawn by a large dog and a boy, who walked along the bank of the canal.

When the boat was in front of Elder Brewster's house, it stopped. The father came ashore and tied his boat to a strong post, and then went back to his breakfast.

This was not served in the neat little cabin with the white curtains in the windows. The breakfast table was spread on the deck of the boat. There was no cloth, but the table was scoured as white as Katrina's strong little arms could make it.

While Katrina and her mother were washing the dishes, the water barge was seen coming slowly down the canal, stopping at each house. The mother saw the little barge, and, calling her son, said something to him which the little Pilgrims could not understand.

But Jan understood. He took up a large, shining can and came over where Jonathan and Patience were.

"Good morning," said Jonathan, "Are you waiting for the water barge, too?" But Jan only smiled and said nothing. He had not understood one word.

When Marion Vedder came up in her flat little boat, with its rows of shining brass water cans, Jan talked fast enough. He seemed to know Marion Vedder, and Karl and Hans, who had come with their mother to help steer the boat.

How fast they all talked, and how strange the language sounded to the English children! The Dutch language was so different from their own. The little Pilgrims thought they could never learn to speak or understand this strange tongue.

But they did, and Jan and Katrina were their first teachers. After a few days, when Jan called in Dutch, "Can you come up on the boat to play?" the English children would answer, "Yes," or "No," in his language.

They soon learned the Dutch names for the games they played, for the different parts of the boat, and for many things in their own homes. Little by little they grew to understand what their neighbors said to them. The children learned the language much more easily than their parents did.

Jan and Katrina lived on the canal boat winter and summer. They had no other home, and they did not wish for one. They thought a canal boat much better than a house, which must always stay in one place.

Many families lived in their boats all of the year. In winter they had to live in the little cabin, but in summer the kitchen, dining room, and sitting room were all on deck.

All Hollanders are fond of flowers and you are sure to see them somewhere around each home. Of course Katrina had her little flower garden. It was in one corner of the deck, and her mother had a long box of plants in the cabin window.

All fall and winter this canal boat stayed in the same place. While their father worked in the mill, Jan and Katrina went to school. Katrina often knitted as she walked to and from school. Little Dutch girls often knit on the street. They can knit and walk as easily as we can talk and walk.

The Weekly Scrubbing Day

Early one morning soon after the Pilgrims came to Holland they heard strange sounds in the street. Such a splashing and dashing of water! Swish! swish! trickle! trickle!

Could it be that the dike was leaking? Mary Chilton ran to the door to see what was the matter.

There she saw Mevrow van Zant and her daughter with jars, and pails, and kettles of water. With her strong white arms the girl dashed the water upon the sides of the house. With long-handled brushes she and her mother scrubbed the windows and walls. Then Hilda dashed on more water and they scrubbed again.

Splash! dash! swish! drip!

How the windows shined! No one could find a spot of dust on that house, if they tried!

Then out came more pails and kettles of water, and more plump Hollanders in their white caps, short skirts, and wooden shoes. All up and down the street, on both sides of the canal, it was, splash! dash! swish! drip!

Even the canal boats were having a wonderful scrubbing, both inside and outside. Their brass trimmings were polished like gold.

While Mary Chilton looked on with wonder in her round eyes, her father came out of the house.

"Why so sober, little one?" he asked. "I think they will not dash water over you."

"I was wondering if our houses are the only ones on the street left dirty, or if we had the only clean ones before. I do not see any dust."

"Oh, that makes no difference," laughed her father. "On scrubbing day, Holland scrubs. It comes so often things never have time to get very dusty."

A Little Milk Peddler

In a cottage near the Pilgrims lived Mevrow van Zant and her three children. Karl was twelve years old and did not like being called a child. Had he not been "mother's right-hand man" all these long weeks while his father was away in his fishing boat? And did he not peddle milk every day to earn money for the family?

Karl had two trusty dogs, and every morning he harnessed them to a little cart. Into the cart he put three shining kettles filled with milk and a long-handled dipper to measure it. Sometimes there were round, yellow cheeses or golden balls of butter to put into the cart, for people were always glad to buy Mevrow's butter and cheese.

The little Pilgrim boys liked to go with Karl when he peddled milk. They liked to help him harness the dogs, and when the cart was ready, away they would all go over the rough stone street. It was hard to tell which made the most noise, Karl's wooden shoes, the heavy wheels of the cart, or the clanging of the milk kettles as they bumped together.

The dogs knew where to take the milk almost as well as Karl did. They stood very still while he went to the door. Often as Karl raised his hand to rap, the door opened, for the good housewife had seen him in her looking-glass. Many of the Dutch women had two looking-glasses just outside their windows. In them they could see far up and down the street without leaving their chairs.

There was at least one pair of wooden shoes on nearly every doorstep, for the children of Holland were taught to take off their shoes before they went into the house.

One morning there was a pretty blue pincushion on the door of a house where Karl and Jonathan Brewster left milk. It was made of silk and trimmed with ribbon and lace.

"What a strange place for a pincushion!" exclaimed Jonathan.

"Don't you know what that means? The storks have brought a baby girl to this house," answered Karl.

"The storks!" exclaimed Jonathan, in surprise.

"The storks, of course," answered Karl. "If you are kind to the storks, and never hurt them or say bad things about them, they will bring you all sorts of enjoyment. Perhaps they will like you well enough to build a nest on your chimney. If you nail a cartwheel across the largest chimney, it will make a better place for a nest."

"There goes a stork now, with a frog in its mouth. As he flies he looks like a great goose except for those long legs stretched out behind him," said Jonathan.

"Oh, he is much larger than a goose, and his bill is three times as long."

"Are storks as good to eat as geese?" asked Jonathan.

"To eat! Eat a stork!" cried Karl, in horror. "We would not kill a stork for anything. Did I not tell you storks bring us enjoyment?"

"It would be enjoyable to get such a big bird if it tasted as good as Christmas goose," replied Jonathan.

"Greedy! It would be the last good luck you would ever have," answered the little Hollander.

"Pooh!" said Jonathan, ""My father says there is no such thing as luck, for it is God who controls all of the events of life."

"Just let me tell you what happened to Jacob Pelton," said Karl. "For two hours he had sat on the dike with his rod and line and had caught only three little fish, so Jacob was very upset.

"Just as he came up to his house with his basket on his arm, down flew one of the storks which lived on his chimney. I suppose the stork had not had good luck with his fishing, either, and his babies and their mother were hungry.

"When the stork saw Jacob's basket of fish he put in his long bill and helped himself to the largest one there. Oh, how angry Jacob was! Before the stork had time to spread his wings, Jacob struck him with his staff. I am sure he did not mean to kill the bird, but there he lay dead.

"And now listen," said Karl, in a low voice. "That very week the cows got in and ate up all of his garden. Then little Peter fell off the dike and broke his arm. Not long after that Jacob lost his job in the mill. He has had bad luck ever since he killed that stork."

"I do not believe the storks had a thing to do with it," said Jonathan, when the story was ended.

"You just ask anybody in Amsterdam whether storks bring luck," answered Karl.

"You have a nest of storks on your chimney. What good luck did they ever bring you?" asked Jonathan.

"Oh, we are always lucky," answered Karl. "Every season father catches a great boat load of fish. We can always sell our milk and vegetables, butter and cheese. We are almost always well, and all last year I stood at the head of my class at school. Yes, the storks have brought us much good luck."

"I do not believe in storks, anyway," insisted the little Christian English boy.

"Hush!" whispered Karl. "You had better not let the storks hear you say that."

Comprehension Questions

1. What pulled Karl's milk cart?

2. Why were there wooden shoes by the doorsteps?

3. What did some of the Dutch people think about the storks that Jonathan knew was not true?

STREET IN HOLLAND.

Winter in Holland

When the days grew shorter and cooler there were no baby storks in their homes on the chimney tops. Those that were little birdlings when the Pilgrims went to Holland had grown large and strong. For weeks their parents had taken them on long flights into the country, that their wings might grow strong for a longer journey.

Still the days grew shorter. The cold north wind blew off the sea. Even the nest on the chimney was no longer comfortable.

The storks knew it was time to fly to their winter home in the far south. So they spread their wings and away they flew in long lines across the sky, hundreds and thousands of them.

Then came a still, cold night, and a day just as cold. There were no little girls knitting on the street that day. Their fingers were hidden in warm red mittens, and they hurried home as fast as their wooden shoes would carry them.

Boys swung their arms to keep warm, and talked of the fun there would be on the ice if it stayed cold until tomorrow. There would be no school, and the stores and mills would be closed, for the first day of skating is a holiday in Holland.

The next morning the Pilgrims were awakened at daybreak by merry shouts on the canal. Bartholomew

Allerton ran to the window, but the frost on the panes was so thick he could not see out. He breathed upon the glass and scraped away some of the frost. Down the canal came eight boys in a row, each holding to the jacket of the boy in front of him. They flew past the house like a flash of light.

Bartholomew could hardly wait to eat his breakfast, he was so eager to go out upon the canal. Suppose we put on our skates and go with him.

What a merry place the canal is this morning! Everybody is on skates today. Here come three market women from the country. Each has on her shoulders a wooden yoke from which hang baskets of vegetables. There is a man with a yoke, too. He must have milk in those bright cans. I am afraid it will freeze if he has far to go.

Just see Marion Vetter! What is she carrying on her back? Oh, it is her baby in a snug little nest made of his mother's shawl. He puts his arms around her neck and she holds his little hands. He is warm and happy, and he coos and chatters, trying to tell her about the people he sees on the canal. He thinks skating is great fun.

There goes Doctor Fuller, skating to see a sick man at the other end of town. At the rate he goes he will soon be there. And who is this pushing a sled before him as he skates? Bartholomew knows him. That is Peter Houten with his lame sister. She cannot skate, so Peter has fixed her chair on a sled and covered it with warm fur. On the sled is a little foot stove filled with hot coals, so she will not get cold. Her pale cheeks have grown rosy and her eyes shine with pleasure.

Now we have come to the great canal beyond the city. It is much wider than the others. Here are beautiful sleighs drawn by horses, their bells making merry music on the canal.

There is a group of boys on skates, playing the game boys play all the world over. They hit a ball with their clubs and away it flies over the smooth ice. Look out, boys! See these white sails flying down the canal. Whoever saw a sleepy canal boat go so fast! Has it too put on skates?

Whiz! Whir-r-r! It is past. What was it? Look out! Here comes another! Whir-r! Whiz! Whir-r-r!

They are ice boats and have runners like a sled. The wind fills their sails and they go faster than a ship on the water, faster than the swiftest horse. They are too dangerous to run on the crowded canals in the city. They must stay on the lakes, or river, or on the great canals outside of the town. Even here they must stay on their own side of the canal and we must stay on ours, or some one will be hurt.

Comprehension Exercise

Copy only the true sentences.

1. The storks flew south to their winter homes.

2. Children would swim in the canals.

3. The first day of skating was a holiday.

4. A doctor skated over to see a sick man.

5. Even a dog was on skates.

6. A boy was pushing a sled with his lame sister on it.

7. Ice boats had runners like sleds.

From Amsterdam to Leiden

A few miles away from Amsterdam is the beautiful city of Leiden, with its many water-streets, fine schools, and great woolen and linen mills. For many reasons this city seemed to the Pilgrims a better place than Amsterdam to make their homes.

So one spring morning a little fleet of canal boats sailed up to the street where the Pilgrims all lived. It did not take them long to load their goods upon the boats, for they had very little. They were much poorer than they had been in England, but they were not unhappy.

When all was ready, the square, brown sails were raised and the boats moved slowly down the canal between the rows of houses and trees. At every cross street the bridge must be raised to allow them to pass.

From one little canal into another they sailed, until the city was left behind. Then they passed into the great, broad canal which lay across the country from city to city. It looked like a long, bright ribbon stretched across the green meadows.

It was a trip long to be remembered. Behind them were the shining waters of the sea and the spires of the city they were leaving.

On both sides were rich, green meadows and herds of fine black and white cattle. There were many beautiful ponds and lakes, and pretty little summerhouses brightly painted.

Whichever way the Pilgrims looked they could see the large windmills. Sometimes they stood in groups, looking like a family of giants against the sky. Here and there one stood so close to the canal that the Pilgrims could see the flowers in the windows of the first story, where the miller's family lived. They could even speak to the miller's children, who played about the door or helped their father load the bags of meal into his boat.

But these windmills were not all used to grind grain into meal. Some were sawmills; others pumped water out of the low meadows into the canal. The canals flowed between thick stone walls and were high above the fields about them.

Sometimes the Pilgrims passed gardens of bright flowers. These were tulip farms where thousands of these bright flowers were raised.

There is no flower so dear to the hearts of the Hollanders as the tulip. There was once a time when they seemed to think more of these bright blossoms than of anything else. They sold houses and lands, cattle and horses, to buy a few tulip bulbs. They were more precious than jewels. A thousand dollars was not thought too great a price for the finest plants.

But when the Pilgrims were in Holland the "tulip craze" had not yet begun. I think the Hollanders enjoyed their beds of common tulips more than they did the few costly blossoms they bought later. If a few of the common tulips died then there was no great loss.

As the Pilgrims came nearer the city of Leiden, they saw a strange sight. Close beside a large garden of bright flowers was a field which looked as if it were covered with deep snow. They could see it was not a field of white flowers. What could it be?

When the boats reached this place, the Pilgrims saw long pieces of white linen bleaching in the sun. They had been woven in one of the mills at Leiden.

Late in the afternoon the great stone wall around the city came in sight. Above it rose the roofs of buildings, church spires, and the beautiful bell tower of the statehouse.

As the band of Pilgrims sailed through the water-gates into the city, the chimes in the tower began to ring. To the Pilgrims they seemed to say, "Welcome to Leiden! Welcome to Leiden!"

A HIGHWAY IN HOLLAND.

In Leiden

Before bringing their families to Leiden, the Pilgrim men had all found work in that city. A few of them worked in the printing shops, but most of them went to the great woolen mills.

Here some washed the wool, or combed it ready for the spinning wheels. Some dyed it, some wove it into cloth. Others packed the finished cloth in boxes, or loaded it on ships.

This work was very different from anything they had done in England. There they had been farmers, working in the fresh air and sunshine on their own fields. At first the work in the mills seemed very hard to them, but they worked early and late, hoping to earn enough to buy little farms sometime.

The Pilgrims had no church of their own when they went to Leiden, but John Robinson, their pastor, had a large house, and they all went there to worship.

There was no reason for secret meetings in Holland. As long as they were honest and well behaved, no one cared how the newcomers worshiped. So every Sunday morning, when the bells in the great church towers rang, the Pilgrims walked to Master Robinson's house.

Near their pastor's home was the largest and finest church in Leiden. As they walked to meeting, they met hundreds of good Hollanders in their finest suits and silver buckles, or fullest skirts and prettiest lace caps, going to church.

Across her forehead nearly every woman wore a beautifully carved band of gold, which ended in large, round buttons above her ears. From these great gold buttons hung long earrings which almost touched her shoulders. The little girls dressed much like their mothers, except that their headdress was more simple. Sometimes their little wooden shoes were prettily carved with leaves and blossoms.

At first, as they passed, these people looked with wonder at the Pilgrims. Their plain brown or gray dress, their high hats, or simple little caps looked very odd to the Hollanders who were so fond of bright colors and pretty clothes. But soon they felt acquainted with their new neighbors and nodded to them pleasantly when they met.

A number of strangers came to John Robinson's meeting one morning. Some of these strangers were English people who had not come from Scrooby. Some were from France, where their king had treated them as cruelly as King James had treated the Pilgrims.

Among them were Master and Mistress Mullens, and their two children, Joseph and Priscilla. Joseph was a frail little fellow and very timid. Priscilla was a rosy-cheeked, merry little girl with sunny hair and laughing eyes.

Master Robinson and the other Pilgrims were glad to have these people join them. They made them very welcome.

How happy they all were as they sang their songs of praise and listened to their pastor's voice. No more hiding from the soldiers; no more dark, damp prisons. Those sad days were gone forever.

A Perplexing Problem

When they first came to Holland, everything seemed strange to the English children. The bright-colored houses with their floors of blue tile, their strange little fireplaces, and their steep roofs, were very different from the homes they had left in England.

They had never seen wooden shoes such as the Dutch children wore. The dikes to keep out the sea, the giant windmills, and the canals all seemed odd.

Strangest of all was the language. They thought they could never learn it.

But after they had lived in Holland a few years these things did not seem so strange. The little English children began to like the Dutch dress and ways. They liked the canal streets, the whirling windmills, and the Dutch cottages.

They liked the pretty, bright dresses and gold cap-buttons which the Dutch girls wore. They sometimes coaxed their mothers to wear pretty lace caps and fine earrings such as their neighbors wore.

"It is not right for you to care so much about pretty clothes," said their parents. "Plain caps and dresses are more suitable for Pilgrims."

These children soon learned the language of Holland, and liked it almost as well as their native one. Indeed, some of them liked it better and often spoke Dutch at home instead of English.

It was now eleven years since the Pilgrims had come to Holland. In this time many babies had been born in their new homes. When these little ones began to talk, their parents taught them to speak English, but when they were old enough to play out of doors, they heard Dutch all around them, and when they went to school they heard nothing but that language. Soon the little ones were speaking better Dutch than English.

This was a real sorrow to the Pilgrim fathers and mothers, who did not want their children to become Hollanders. They wished them to remember the English language and English ways. They feared that in a few years no one could tell their children from those of the Hollanders.

The Pilgrims often talked about their old homes in England. Many of them were not so well and strong since they worked in the mills. Worst of all, many of their children had to work there while they were still young. Their rosy cheeks were growing pale, and their backs bent.

The Pilgrims longed for little farms of their own, where they and their sons could work in the open air as they had done in England, but they were too poor to buy farms in Holland.

"We hear much about the new land across the sea," said John Robinson, their pastor. "A good many Englishmen have gone there and made comfortable homes for themselves. They say it is a great, beautiful country where there is land enough for all."

"I am told the ground there is very rich, and the crops never fail for want of rain or sunshine," said John Carver.

"If we were in America we could make homes such as we had in England. We could have our own church, and bring up our children to love and serve God," said Elder Brewster.

"Can we go so far away?" they thought. Between America and Holland the sea is very wide.

The Pilgrims thought of the pleasant homes and the dear friends they would leave in Holland. They thought how long it would be before they could have homes as good as those in Leiden.

They thought of the long voyage, and of the hardships of life in the new land. There was not a city, nor a town, nor even a house in the place where they would go. There were no mills where they could buy timber for their cottages. They would have to cut down the trees to make their own lumber.

"The Indians live in the forests. They are said to be very savage and cruel," said Master Allerton.

"We would treat them like brothers and perhaps they would be our friends," answered the pastor.

Whenever the Pilgrims met they talked about going to America. They talked about the broad fields they would own, and the cozy homes they would build.

"Above all," they said, "we shall be free. We will build our own church and worship God as the Bible directs. Our children will be healthier, happier, and holier than in this large city."

And so the Pilgrims decided to go to America. But they could not all go at once. There would be no houses for them to live in at first, and many were too old, or too weak, to bear the hardships of starting the new home.

It was decided that if the greater number of the Pilgrims went to America, John Robinson would go with them. If fewer went, Elder Brewster would go with them and be their pastor. It was soon learned that most of them could not leave Leiden until later, so Elder Brewster and about eighty of his friends planned to go that summer.

Only those who were well and strong were to go in the first ship. Many families would have to be separated for a year or more.

Elder Brewster's family was large, and he could not take them all at first. Love and her little brother were too young to be left. Mistress Brewster could not be contented an hour if the wide sea lay between her and her little boys.

Jonathan Brewster was a young man now, and was working in Leiden. Patience and Fear had grown to be tall girls, and could spin and weave, sew and cook almost as well as Mistress Brewster herself.

So it was arranged that Jonathan would go on with his work in Leiden, with his sisters to keep house for him. They all hoped to be able to join the others in America in a year or two.

Comprehension Questions

1. When the Pilgrims first came to Holland, how did the way of living there seem to them?

2. What was happening to the ways the English children talked and wanted to dress as they lived in this Dutch country?

3. Where did the English people begin thinking would be a good place to live?

4. What was the most important reason for moving to this new country?

STANDISH AND HIS COMPANIONS.

The Sword of Miles Standish

Among those who went to John Robinson's church was Captain Miles Standish. He was an Englishman, but he had lived many years in Holland, where he went to help the Dutch fight for their freedom.

Once while he was fighting in Holland, some soldiers went to the house of an old man who made swords and armor. They took some of the armor and were threatening to harm the old man and his daughter.

Captain Standish saw them, and shouted, "You cowards! To steal from a poor old man! Cowards! Give back everything you have taken." And the rude soldiers obeyed.

Then to the trembling old man he said, "No harm shall come to you, so do not be afraid. Your life is safe, and your daughter, too, is free from danger. Go back to your shop in peace."

The old man could not thank him then; his heart was too full. But that night Miles Standish heard a knock at his door. When he looked out he saw the old sword maker standing in the darkness. He had something carefully wrapped in his cloak.

"Captain Standish," he said, "you are a brave, brave soldier. You are more than that; you are a kind and noble man." Then, holding out the gift he had brought, the man said, "Take this sword and take with it the heartfelt thanks of an old man whose life and whose daughter you have saved."

Miles Standish could not refuse without giving pain, so he took the man's gift. It was a fine old sword which had been made in the Far East hundreds of years before Miles Standish was born. On one side were engraved the sun, moon, and stars. On the other side were some words written in an old, old language.

The Captain thanked the man and said, "This sword shall always be my friend. It shall always be ready to help those who are in trouble." He named the sword "Gideon," and he sometimes spoke to it as though it were a friend.

But now the war was over, and though it had been ten years since Miles Standish had needed "Gideon," it always hung at his side.

Captain Standish often talked with the Pilgrims about their plan of going to America. He thought about the Indian warriors who lived in the new land, and about the ships from other countries which might try to take their town.

"I will go with you to your new home," he said. "There may be work for 'Gideon' and me."

Preparing for the Journey

That spring brought very busy days to the Pilgrims in Leiden. Those who were going to America had many things to prepare and those who stayed behind were glad to help them get ready.

They must have plenty of cloth made, for there would be no time to weave more until their new homes were built. It would be a cold winter by that time and they must have warm jackets, and dresses, and cloaks.

So hum-m-m! hum-m-m! went the spinning wheels from morning till night. And click! clack! click! clack! went the big looms, as the flying shuttle wove the gray yarn into cloth.

Far into the night the tired women stitched with busy fingers. In those days all the sewing had to be done by hand, and it took much time and much patient labor to make a garment.

There was plenty of work for the children as well as for their elders. Even tiny hands could hold the thread while mother wound the yarn into a ball. And you should have seen the dozens of thick, warm mittens and stockings that were knit by little hands that summer.

The Pilgrims could not take any cows with them, so in every cottage there were small tubs being packed with sweet, yellow butter to be taken to the new homes across the sea.

TWO MEN BRING A CASK ON BOARD.

It would take them many weeks to cross the ocean, and much food would be needed for the journey. They could not raise more grain until the next summer, so they must take enough to last them all winter.

With the money the Pilgrims had given him, Elder Brewster had bought a small ship in Holland. It was called the *Speedwell*, and it now waited for them at Delfshaven, about twenty-four miles away.

If you had been in Leiden one morning late in July, you might have seen the Pilgrims loading the canal boats which would carry them to Delfshaven. Almost before it was light that morning the men began to carry things upon the boats. Their kind Dutch neighbors worked as busily as they, helping to carry the heavy boxes of ship bread, salted meats, or dried fruits.

There were barrels and barrels of meal, and other barrels holding grain for seed. There were great sacks of beans, dried peas, and vegetables, but at last the boats were loaded.

The Pilgrims had many friends in England who they thought would like to go to America with them. So Elder Brewster had gone to England to see them, and to arrange for a ship to carry them all across the sea.

He was gone several weeks, and when he returned he found the Pilgrims ready for the journey. Each family could take only a few of the most needed things. There would not be room on the ship for all their goods, so they would take only such things as they could not make.

The beautiful china plates and cups they had bought in Holland must be left, for they would be easily broken. Their old pewter dishes would last much longer, and they would look very well when they were scoured bright with sand.

They would take their silver spoons and the steel knives they had brought from England. The old brass candlesticks, the spinning wheels, and the great copper kettles must have a place in the boat.

Comprehension Questions

1. What were the women busy making for those who would be going to America?

2. What ship were they planning to take from Holland?

3. List four kinds of food they had packed in barrels to take.

4. List three of the items they took.

Farewell to Holland

When all was ready, they bade their Dutch friends good-bye. How kind these people had been to them during the years they had lived in Holland. They had done all they could to make the Pilgrims happy and comfortable in their city. And when they were preparing to go away, many yellow balls of cheese, little tubs of butter, and webs of white linen came from these good Hollanders.

John Robinson and all the members of his church went to Delfshaven with those who were to sail on the *Speedwell*.

As the canal boats moved slowly away, the Pilgrims looked for the last time upon their little cottages. They had lived twelve long years in Holland, and it seemed like a dear home to them. Most of the children had never known any other home.

Groups of Hollanders stood at their doors to wave farewell to the Pilgrims as they passed. Five or six little boys with bare legs and clumsy wooden shoes, ran along beside the canal boats, calling in Dutch to their friends.

But now the boys had shouted a last "good-bye;" the city with its great mills and shops, its quaint houses and pretty gardens lay behind them. They were coming to the beautiful city gate with its round towers and pointed spires.

Mary Chilton and Fear and Patience Brewster stood together looking at the large gate. "Do you remember the

first time we passed through this gate, Mary?" asked
Patience. "That was eleven years ago and you were a very
little girl then."

"Yes, indeed, I remember it," answered Mary. "I was six
years old. I can remember our home in England and the
ship in which we came to Holland. Can you, Fear?"

"I do not remember much about England," answered Fear,
who was the youngest of the three, "but I remember our
home in Amsterdam. I wonder where Jan and Katrina
are this summer. Their boat was in Leiden all winter."

And so the girls talked of anything except the long
parting. They could not speak of that. The tears were so
close to Fear's eyes she was afraid to blink lest they run
over.

This was a beautiful summer day. Holland meadows had
never looked brighter. There were charming little
summerhouses perched on stilts by the side of the lake.
Some stood in the water and a little boat tied to the steps
of one showed how its owner had reached it. There he sat
smoking his long pipe and watching his little son, who sat
on the doorstep and fished.

Everywhere were the windmills, the dikes, and the canals
that had seemed so strange to them at first. Now all these
things seemed like old friends to the Pilgrims and made
them sad to say good-bye to Holland.

Late in the evening they reached Delfshaven, where the
Speedwell was waiting for them. All night the sailors

worked, loading the goods from the canal boats into the ship, and making ready for an early start in the morning.

Then came the hardest parting. The tears would start. Even strong men wept as they looked into each other's faces and thought that perhaps they might never see these friends again.

There on the ocean shore these brave men and women knelt down and prayed to the God they loved. They prayed that He would be with those who stayed as well as with those who sailed away. Their pastor's voice broke many times as he spoke to God of his friends.

After this prayer, the Pilgrims went silently and sadly on board the *Speedwell* and sailed away to England. They waved to the dear ones on the shore and stood watching them as long as they could be seen.

Comprehension Exercise

1. Write a couple of sentences to tell why it was so difficult for the Pilgrims to say farewell to their Dutch friends.

The *Speedwell*

Four days of good wind and fair weather brought the *Speedwell* to England. There the Pilgrims found about forty friends who wished to go with them to America. They had hired a little ship called the *Mayflower*, which now lay in the harbor ready to sail. It, too, was loaded with provisions for the long journey and the cold winter.

The *Speedwell* was a smaller vessel than the *Mayflower*, so some of the Pilgrims from Holland joined their friends on the larger boat. Then the two ships sailed out of the harbor into the blue sea.

The Pilgrims watched the shores of their native land grow fainter. Would they ever see dear old England again? Surely none expected to see it so soon as they did.

They were hardly out of sight of land when the *Speedwell* began to leak. They could see no hole, but slowly the water rose in the bottom of the boat. It crept around the boxes and barrels stored there. "The hole must be behind this pile of boxes," said the captain.

While some of the men pumped the water out of the ship, others quickly moved the great boxes away.

Yes, there was a little stream of water running down from a hole in the side of the ship. This was soon mended, but still the water slowly rose in the boat. The men at the pumps worked harder than ever, but the water came in as fast as they could pump it out.

More holes were found and mended, but still the ship leaked. There was nothing to do but go back to land as soon as possible. Those on the *Mayflower* did not wish to go on without their friends, so both ships returned to England. When the *Speedwell* reached shore, the ship builders came to look at it.

"It carries too heavy a mast for so small a ship," said one.

"The hull is worn out," said another. "See, it needs new boards, and fresh tar, and fresh paint. It will take weeks to repair this ship and make it safe for so long a voyage."

What could the Pilgrims do? The fine weather was passing. They would hardly reach America now before the heavy storms of winter came. It was quite plain they could not wait until the *Speedwell* was repaired.

The *Mayflower* could not hold all who wished to go to America, yet the Pilgrims could not hire another ship. The passengers on the *Speedwell* were a long way from home. It seemed hard for them to return to Holland.

So some of those who lived in England offered to give up their places in the *Mayflower* and return to their homes.

"Next summer there will be other ships sailing to America from England, and it may be a long time before another will go from Holland," they said.

Comprehension Exercise

Find answers from your story to fill in the blanks.

1. After _____ days the Pilgrims came to England on the *Speedwell*.

2. About _____ friends wanted to go to America, too.

3. They had hired a little ship called the _____.

4. Both ships came back to England because the *Speedwell* began to _____.

5. The Pilgrims wanted to hurry and leave before the _____ storms came.

6. Because everyone could not fit on the *Mayflower*, some would try to go next _____.

The Voyage of the *Mayflower*

When the provisions and the boxes of other goods had been moved from the *Speedwell* to the larger boat, the *Mayflower* started once more. Now she carried a hundred passengers besides her sailors.

By today's standards, the *Mayflower* was a very small boat in which to cross the ocean. The cabin was badly crowded, and there was only one small deck.

At that time no one had thought of making a boat go by steam or diesel. The *Mayflower* had large white sails, and when the wind was good she sped over the water like a great sea bird.

But sometimes there was no wind, and the little vessel lay still upon the quiet water. Sometimes the sky grew black with storm clouds and the fierce winds swept down upon the ship. Then the sailors quickly bound the sails close to the masts, but still the vessel was often driven far off of her course. No wonder it took so long to cross the ocean in those days.

In one of these great storms a young man almost lost his life. For many days the passengers had been kept in the cabin by the weather. The deck was wet and slippery. The rough winds swept across it; the waves washed over it. It was not safe for any of the passengers there.

But John Howland did not like to stay quietly in the crowded cabin. So he climbed the narrow stairs and stepped out upon the slippery deck.

How wild and terrible the storm was! The waves were almost as high as the masts! Sometimes the *Mayflower* rode high upon the tops of the waves. At other times it was quite hidden between them.

John saw a great wave about to break over the ship. He tried to reach the cabin door, but was too late. With a crash like thunder, the wave struck the ship and swept away one of the masts. John seized the railing with both hands, but the wave was stronger than he. It flung him into the sea.

"Help! Oh, help!" he cried. "Help!"

But his voice could not be heard above the storm. He fought with the waves and tried to swim, but it was of no use. The water closed over his head. Who could help him now?

Over the side of the ship hung some ropes dragged down by the falling mast. John saw one of these long ropes trailing through the water. The rope was close at hand, and he reached out and grasped it.

Hand over hand, he pulled himself toward the ship. His strength was fading fast. Would no one come to his rescue?

Some sailors on the *Mayflower* saw John struggling for his life. "Hold on, John!" they shouted, as they pulled in the rope.

John did hold on, though his hands were stiff with cold, and the waves beat him back from the ship. Slowly he was lifted from the water, and strong arms reached down to help him. At last he lay upon the deck, faint but safe.

Comprehension Exercises

Copy the sentences that are true about your story.

1. The *Mayflower* was a very large ship.

2. The ship moved when wind blew the sails.

3. The sails had to be taken down when a storm began.

4. Many people saw John Howland fall in the ocean.

5. John grabbed a rope hanging from the ship.

Water Babies

On and on the ship sailed. How wide the water seemed.

Some days were full of sunshine; the little children could play upon the deck. They loved to watch the sunset across the wide ocean. Then the sky was bright with purple and gold. Each wave caught the colors from the clouds until the whole world seemed aglow.

They loved to watch the stars come out in the evening. At first only two or three of the biggest, bravest ones peeped forth, to see if the sun had gone. Then a few others looked timidly out. Yes, the sun was really gone, and his glory of red and gold was quickly following him.

Then troops of little stars burst from their hiding places. They twinkled merrily at the little Pilgrims, as if to say, "See we are going with you to your new home. We went with you to Holland; we will go with you to America. Do not be lonely."

But it grew colder, for the winter was drawing near. Many days the deck was too cold and icy to play upon. Then the children must stay in the dark, crowded cabin.

Poor little Pilgrims! Many were ill, and all wished the long voyage would end. There were but few games they could play in the little cabin, and they had no toys or story books. How they longed for the green fields and shady woods!

Then Priscilla told them stories of the sunny land where she once lived. Did only pleasant things happen in that wonderful country? If there were any unhappy times there, Priscilla never spoke of them. The stories she told were such merry tales they brought sunshine into the gloomiest little faces.

Even tired mothers, who were too far away to hear the story, would smile as they looked into Priscilla's laughing eyes. "What a comfort that child is," they often said.

Then Mary Chilton, who had grown to be a tall girl now, played games with them. John Alden whittled out a wonderful puzzle for them, and everyone tried to make the voyage pleasant.

But nine weeks is a long time to be shut up on a boat, and be tossed about by the rough waves. The little ones were so tired, it seemed to them they could not stand it any longer.

Then what do you think happened way out there on the ocean? Two dear little baby boys were born. Oh, how happy the children were! They forgot to be tired then.

You may be sure those babies never lacked nurses. It was such fun to hold them and sing to them softly until they closed their eyes and went to sleep.

Of course, every one wanted to help name the babies. Each thought of the very best name he knew, but it was hard to suit all.

Giles Hopkins wished to name his baby brother Jan, after a friend in Holland but that name did not suit his parents at all. They did not want to give their baby a Dutch name.

Mistress Hopkins thought he should be named Stephen for his father.

"No," said Master Hopkins, "if he were given my name he would be called 'little Stephen' until he grew to be a man. I believe no child was ever born here before. I wish he might have a name no other has ever had."

What could it be? Some spoke of *Mayflower*, but others thought that a better name for a little girl.

A week passed and still the baby was not named. "This will never do," said his mother. "Constance, you have not said what you would like to name your little brother."

Constance said she had been thinking "Ocean" would be a good name for this baby.

"Ocean! - Ocean!" whispered the mother to herself. It was certainly a very suitable name, but it had a strange sound. Surely no other child had ever borne that name.

When Elder Brewster heard about the new name he said, "I know of a word in another language which means ocean. It is Oceanus. Perhaps you would like that name better."

"Oceanus!" That seems like an unusual name for a child, but the Pilgrims often gave their children names which seem strange to us. This did not sound so strange to them. They thought "Oceanus Hopkins" a very good name for the baby, and so it was decided.

Then came the other wee baby. He too must have a suitable name. What should it be?

After many names had been considered, Mary Allerton said she thought "Wandering" would be a good name for the baby, because the Pilgrims were wandering in search of a home.

Mistress White did not quite like "Wandering" for a name, but she asked Elder Brewster if he did not know another word which meant the same thing.

And so this baby was named "Peregrine." Peregrine White and Oceanus Hopkins! "Those are very large names for such very tiny babies," thought little Love Brewster.

Comprehension Questions

1. Why could the children not play on the deck as winter drew near?

2. What did Priscilla do to help the time pass for the children?

3. What did Mary do with them?

4. What names were given to the two babies who were born on the ship?

5. Do you think it was easy for any of the people as they traveled?

Land

It was now nine weeks since the Pilgrims sailed from England. No one had thought the voyage would be so long. The captain felt sure they must be coming near land, but he could not tell just where they were.

Many times a day, a sailor climbed high up on the mast to look for land. Still there was nothing to be seen but the wide sea, not an island, nor even a ship.

At daybreak one cold November morning, a glad shout rang through the ship. "Land! Land!"

Yes, there lay the land - that new land which was to be their home and ours.

There were no rocky cliffs like those of England. Before them rose tall, green pine trees, and great oaks still wearing their dress of reddish brown.

Not a town or a single house could they see. No smoke rose from the forest to tell them where a village lay hidden. Not a sound was heard but the whistling of the cold wind through the ropes and masts, and the lapping of the water around the boat.

"This is not the sunny southland we had hoped to find," said their governor, John Carver. "The storms have driven us too far north for that."

"No, this is not the sunny southland, but land of any sort is a joyful sight after our long voyage," replied Elder Brewster. "Let us not forget to thank God, who has brought us safe to this new land."

It was too near winter to sail farther south. Near by the Pilgrims must find the best place to make their home. So the little ship sailed into the quiet bay and dropped anchor. Perhaps it, too, was glad the long voyage was ended.

The water in the bay was so shallow that the ship could not reach the shore. So the men quickly lowered the small boat the *Mayflower* carried. Then Miles Standish, William Bradford, John Alden, and several of the others climbed down the rope ladder into their boat and rowed away. They carried their guns and axes, and had an empty keg which they hoped to fill with fresh water. That which they brought from England was almost gone, and all were thirsty for a drink of cold, fresh water.

The sun had gone under a cloud, and the wind was wild and cold. The icy water dashed over the hands of the men as they rowed. When they reached the shore, they pulled the boat upon the sand that it might not drift away.

"I think two or three men had better stay near the boat while the others go into the forest," said Captain Standish. "We would be in a sad plight if Indians were to steal our boat while we are all gone."

So John Alden and William Bradford stayed near the boat. Floating on the shallow water, or flying through the air, were hundreds of wild fowl. The Pilgrims had not tasted fresh meat since they left England. What a treat some of these wild birds would be!

The two men knelt behind their boat and kept very still. After a while the birds came near to the boat. Bang! Bang! flashed the guns, and bang! - bang! - bang! rang the echo.

Away flew the birds, but John ran along the shore, and waded into the water, picking up the ducks they had killed. "We will have a supper fit for a king tonight," said John to himself, as he carried the birds back to the boat.

Then they built a fire of dry branches, to warm their stiffened fingers and dry their clothes. When the wood was all ablaze they piled green pine branches upon the fire. There was a sharp, crackling sound, and a cloud of black smoke arose.

"If the men get lost in the forest they will see this smoke and know which way to go," thought Bradford, as he piled on the sweet-smelling pine.

Then they cut some dry wood to carry back to the *Mayflower*, for the fuel was all gone, and the cabin was very cold. In the bottom of the boat was a pile of clams which the men had dug from the sand.

It was almost night when Captain Standish and his men came out of the forest. They carried some rabbits, and their keg was full of fresh water which they had found not far from the shore.

All day they had not seen a house or a person. When they reached the top of the hill, one man took a glass and climbed a tall pine tree. He was surprised to see that the ocean lay on both sides of the forest. The land seemed like a long arm stretched into the sea.

This was not a good place to make their home. The harbor was too shallow and there were no rivers or large brooks where they could always get fresh water. The little ponds they had found would dry up in the summer.

The next day was the Sabbath. They would spend it quietly on the ship, and on Monday perhaps they could look farther.

Comprehension Questions

1. How many weeks did the Pilgrims sail on the ship?

2. How did a few men get to shore to look over the land?

3. What did Captain Standish and his men bring from the forest?

4. Why did they think this was not a good place to make their home?

The First Washing Day in New England

It was Monday morning, and the sun was brighter and the weather milder than in weeks before.

The children gazed eagerly toward the shore and thought what fun it would be to have a long run on that smooth, sandy beach, or to hunt for nuts in those great woods. They were so tired of being on the ship.

Just then Mistress Brewster came upon the deck. She shaded her eyes with her hand and looked off across the water. "What a good place to do our washing!" she said, as she gazed at the shore. "Not one proper washing day have we had since we sailed."

It did not take long to get tubs, pails, and everything ready. John Alden and John Howland loaded the things into the boat and rowed the merry party to the shore.

But Mistress Brewster did not forget the children, who looked longingly at the boat as it pulled away. When it came back for its next load, she said kindly, "Come, boys. You shall have your run on the beach. We need your quick feet and strong arms to bring brushwood for our fires. And the girls must come too. They can help spread the clothes upon the bushes to dry.

It seemed so good to be on the ground again. As soon as the boat touched the sand the children sprang ashore and raced each other up and down the beach.

"Let's hunt for nuts under those trees!" cried Love Brewster, and away the boys bounded toward the woods. John Alden shouldered his gun and went with them, for it was not safe for them to go into the forest alone.

The first washing day in New England

In the edge of the woods stood a tall, straight tree. The long scales which curled from its shaggy bark told John Alden it was a hickory tree. Under the tree was a thick carpet of yellow-brown leaves. Under that carpet there must be plenty of sweet nuts.

The boys dragged their feet through the deep leaves, or tossed them aside with their hands. Yes, there lay the white nuts, thousands and thousands of them. The frost had opened their tough, brown coats, but the tree had covered them with a blanket of leaves.

While the boys were gone, the men drove two forked stakes into the hard sand. Across the top of these stakes they placed a long pole from which to hang the great kettles.

Soon the fire was snapping and crackling under the kettles. The flames leaped higher and higher as the children piled dry leaves and branches upon them. Then the water began to simmer and sing.

All the morning the women rubbed and boiled, or rinsed and wrung the clothes. The men were kept busy carrying water and firewood.

By noon the tubs were empty, and as Mary Chilton spread the last little dress to dry, she saw the boat pull away from the *Mayflower*.

"Here comes Priscilla with our dinner!" she cried.

Priscilla was a wonderful cook. Sometimes there was but little to cook, but Priscilla could always make something dainty and good from the plainest food.

Today she had made a great kettle of soup, with vegetables and the broth of the wild birds. How good it smelled as it heated over the fire!

Long before night the clean, fresh clothes were dry and folded away in the tubs and kettles. Then the tired but happy Pilgrims rowed back to the *Mayflower*.

A Wild Land

The next day some of the Pilgrims sailed along the shore for several miles, still looking for a deep, safe harbor and a stream of clear water.

At last they noticed a little brook, and turned their boat toward the shore. Leaving four men to guard the boat, the others struck out into the forest. Not a sound did they hear but the rustling of dry leaves as they walked through them, or the moaning of the wind in the tree tops. The November woods seemed very bare and lonely.

When they had gone a mile or two, they saw a large deer drinking at a brook. They stood still and watched him, but the deer had heard their step. He raised his beautiful head and listened a moment, then bounded swiftly into the forest.

But William Bradford was not watching the deer. His sharp eyes had seen something moving on the hilltop not far away. As he gazed he saw, first the head and shoulders, and then the whole body of a man appear over the brow of the hill. Then came another, and another. Could it be John Alden and the others had left the boat and come after them? Surely they would not disobey the captain, for Miles Standish had told them not to leave the boat lest the Indians take it.

But now he could see their red faces, and their long, black hair and eagle feathers.

"Look!" he whispered, "Indians! Indians!"

"Perhaps that means work for 'Gideon,'" thought Captain Standish, as he seized his sword.

"Put away your sword, Captain," said Governor Carver, gently. "We want to make friends of these people if we can. Perhaps they can tell us of some town or settlement. At least we may be able to buy some food from them."

So the Pilgrims waited quietly in the shadows of the forest until the Indians came near. Down the hill they came, their quick eyes looking for the print of a deer in the soft earth.

When they reached the foot of the hill they saw tracks which had been made by no animal of the forest. Neither had they been made by an Indian's moccasin. There seemed to be hundreds of these tracks. What could it mean? They stood close together and peered eagerly into the forest.

Then the Pilgrims stepped from behind the trees, and came toward them. John Carver, the governor, held out to them some strings of bright beads, but the Indians would have none of them.

For a moment they gazed at the white men in terror. Then without stopping to fit an arrow to their bow strings, they fled.

Where had they gone? Had the earth opened and taken in her frightened children? Only an Indian knows how to disappear so quickly.

"Ugh!" they said, when they were safe away. "Ugh! Palefaces have come!"

The Pilgrims followed the Indians for ten miles, but they did not come within sight of the strangers again all that day, though they often saw the print of their feet.

Sometimes these footprints showed where the Indians had climbed a hill to watch the white men.

When night came, the men found a sheltered place to camp until morning. They built a fire, and while two watched, the others slept.

In the morning they marched on again, going farther south. They saw fields where corn had been raised, but not an Indian, or a house of any kind. No doubt the Indians saw them very often, and knew just where they were all the time.

A little later in the day the Pilgrims came to some strange looking houses. They were round and low, with a small opening for a door; a hole in the top served for a chimney.

The men went from one house to another but could find no one. They knelt down and crawled into the wigwams, but there the fires had burned out many days before.

In the wigwams they found earthen pots and dishes, wooden bowls, and beautiful baskets made of grasses and trimmed with shells. Now they could see that the framework of the wigwam was made of long willow branches with both ends stuck into the ground. Over the frame the Indians had fastened large mats of woven reeds, which kept out the cold and rain. From the inside the wigwam looked like a great open umbrella.

"What is this?" shouted one of the men, as he came upon a little mound of earth near the Indian village.

"Perhaps it is an Indian grave," replied another.

"No, it is too wide and round for that. We will open it and see what is buried here."

So they dug away the earth and found a large basket. It was round and narrow at the top, and was covered with large leaves. After a good deal of trouble the basket was raised from the hole and opened. It was filled to the brim with corn, some white, some red, and some of a bluish color.

This was Indian corn. It did not grow in England or Holland then, and the Pilgrims had never seen grain like it before. It tasted very good, and the Pilgrims were much in need of food. The provisions which they had brought from England were almost gone.

So finally they decided to take back to the *Mayflower* as much corn as they could carry, and pay the Indians for it when they could.

Soon they had dug up about ten bushels of corn. Then they went to the shore and built a fire as a signal for the boat to come for them and take them back to the *Mayflower*.

Comprehension Questions

1. What were the Pilgrims looking for as they sailed along the shore?

2. What did William Bradford see on the hilltop?

3. Why did Governor Carver tell Capt. Standish to put away his sword?

4. Were the Indians happy to see the Pilgrims?

5. What kinds of things did the Pilgrims find in the Indian village?

6. What did the men bring back to the ship?

A Narrow Escape

While the men were away with the boat the children could not go to the shore to play. They had to amuse themselves on the ship as well as they could.

This was not hard for little Francis Billington to do, but his amusements never seemed to please the older people. If he started to cut his name on the railing of the ship, some one was sure to call, "Don't do that!"

If he tried to climb the ropes from the mast, somebody always dragged him down. Even when he sat down quietly to hold one of the babies, it was always, "Francis! See how you let his head hang down," or, "Just look at that baby's little feet! Francis, you must keep them covered." Then some one would come and say, "Let me take the baby. I am so afraid you will drop him."

Poor little Francis! He did not mean to be naughty, but he was a great trial to the Pilgrim mothers and fathers. When he was quiet for a few minutes, they felt sure he must be in some mischief - and they were usually right.

"Francis is not a bad boy," Elder Brewster used to say. "Just wait until his father begins to build his house, then Francis will be too busy to get into mischief. I believe there will not be a harder-working boy in the village than Francis."

"Then let us hurry and find a place to build," said Mistress Billington, "for I am almost worn out."

While his father and the other men were away digging up corn in the Indian village, mischief-loving Francis was wandering about the boat looking for amusement.

In his hands he held some of the pretty feathers of the wild duck. He thought what fun it would be to fill these quills with gunpowder and make some firecrackers. He called them squibs.

So he went down to the cabin where the powder was stored. There was no one in the room, but he soon found a keg which had been opened, and he began to fill his squibs. It was hard to make the powder go into the little quills; most of it went on the floor instead.

When the squibs were filled, he looked about and saw several old muskets hanging upon the wall. "How those women in the next room would jump if I should fire off one of those muskets!" thought the boy.

Muskets made in those days could not be fired by pulling a trigger. The powder must be lighted by a spark of fire. At that time no one had learned how to make matches, either. But Francis knew where to find a slow-burning fuse made of candlewick, and away he ran to get it.

Soon he returned, carrying the burning fuse right into the powder room.

Oh, Francis! Think of the powder upon the floor. And think of that open keg half filled with the deadly powder. If one little spark should reach it, the ship and every one on it would be blown to pieces.

But Francis never stopped to think twice about anything. He climbed upon a box and took down an old musket, then looked to see if it was loaded. Yes, it was all ready to fire, and Francis knew how to do it.

I think the very sun must almost have had a chill when he peeped through the tiny window and saw the terrible danger.

Boom! roared the old musket. Then came a blinding flash, and Boom! Bang! Snap! Crack! Bang! Oh, what a deafening din!

When the thick smoke had cleared a little, a very angry sailor found a very frightened boy in a corner of the cabin. Francis did not know how he came to be lying there in a heap. He only knew that his eyes were smarting and his hands were very sore.

Women with white faces and trembling hands tried to comfort their screaming children. Sailors hurried to and fro looking for leaks in the boat.

But, wonder of wonders, no great harm had been done. The squibs were gone; two or three of the loaded muskets had gone off; but the powder on the floor had flashed up and burned out without setting fire to the keg.

"If that keg had exploded, we should have found no more of the *Mayflower* than a few chips floating upon the water," said Miles Standish, when he heard of it. "I thank God for protecting our ship."

"It was the mercy of God alone," said the Pilgrims.

Comprehension Questions

1. What three things could Francis do that would get him into trouble?

2. How did Elder Brewster feel about Francis?

3. What did Francis call the quills filled with gunpowder?

4. How did muskets have to be fired in those days?

5. Is it dangerous to not think ahead? How was it dangerous in the case of Francis?

6. Why did the Pilgrims say it was God's mercy alone that saved the *Mayflower*?

A Savage Attack

It grew colder and colder every day, but still the Pilgrims had not found a good place to build their homes.

So Governor Carver, William Bradford, Captain Standish, and others again sailed away in their boat. They carried guns and axes, blankets, and food enough to last them many days.

It was December now, and the bay was full of ice. The driving snow and sleet cut their faces and froze on their clothing. Some of the men nearly died of the cold.

Every day they went ashore to see if there was a good place to settle. There were so many things to think about at this time.

They must find a place near the woods so they could get logs for their houses and wood for their fires. Yet the forest must not be too near, for they must have a clear space in which to plant their grain.

There must be a deep, safe harbor, and above all, a stream of clear, fresh water.

They landed again and again, but it was hard to find a place which had all these things. They would search all day and at night make a camp in the forest.

One night after a hard day's tramp, they built a great fire and cooked their supper. They could get plenty of fresh meat in the forest, and they had brought bread, beans, and dried peas from the ship.

After they had eaten their supper and had prayers, all went to sleep except the two men who were to watch.

The light from the flames fell upon the tired faces of the men as they lay in a circle about the fire. It touched lightly the trunks of the tall trees, and stretched long, dark shadows across the hard frozen ground.

Sometimes they saw shining eyes peering at them from the darkness, but the animals were all afraid of the fire and soon slunk away.

About midnight the watchmen heard a long loud cry in the distance. It sounded like the yell of Indians.

"To arms! To arms!" they cried.

The Pilgrims sprang to their feet and seized their guns. A long time they waited and listened, but no Indians came. "Perhaps it was only the howl of wolves or foxes," said the men, as they lay down again.

The Pilgrims were up before the sun, next morning, cooking their breakfast and preparing to sail farther along the shore. While some cooked the meal, others carried blankets and guns down to the boat.

While they were sitting about the fire eating their breakfast, they heard a frightful sound near by.

A Savage Attack

"Woach! Woach! Ha! Ha! Woach!" came the cry.

The Pilgrims sprang to the boat for their guns. They fired several shots into the forest thinking to frighten the Indians, but on they came.

Nearer and nearer sounded the cry. "Woach! Woach! Ha! Ha! Woach!"

In the faint morning light the Pilgrims saw the forms of many Indians slipping from tree to tree. Then whiz! whir! whir! sounded the arrows, as they flew thick and fast. Two of them stuck in John Howland's coat, and one struck Captain Standish above the heart, but he had his armor on and the arrow did no harm.

The Pilgrims quickly sprang away from the light of the fire. They tried to protect themselves in the dark shadows of the forest.

Whiz-z-z! Whir-r-r! The arrows were flying from every direction, but not an Indian was to be seen. They, too, were well hidden behind trees and bushes.

The Pilgrims kept very still. Then the Indians grew bolder. They crept silently toward the camp, their dark forms looking like dim shadows in the forest.

This was just what the Pilgrims were waiting for. Bang! Boom! roared the muskets. One of the bullets struck the Indian chief in the arm. He could not draw his bow again. With an angry yell the warriors fled into the forest.

The Pilgrims followed them a short distance, shouting and firing their muskets. When they returned to the camp, they picked up many arrows. Some were pointed with a sharp bit of deerhorn, and some with eagles' claws. These arrows the Pilgrims sent to England when the *Mayflower* returned.

Comprehension Exercises

Copy only the sentences that are true.

1. The Pilgrims had not yet found a good place to build their homes.

2. They wanted a place where the forest was all around them.

3. The men brought bread, beans and peas from the ship to their camp.

4. About midnight the watchman saw an Indian.

5. John Howland's coat was struck by two arrows.

6. The Pilgrims ran after the Indians deep into the forest.

7. The Pilgrims sent the arrows to England.

Plymouth Bay

A storm of wind and snow came up as the Pilgrims sailed along near the shore. The sea was very rough, and the boat seemed in danger of being upset by the waves which tossed it from side to side. The rudder was broken, and the mast was split in three pieces by the heavy wind.

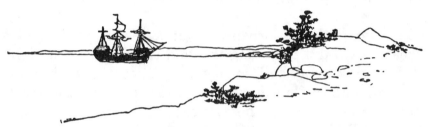

The "Mayflower" in Plymouth Harbor

There was an island near the mouth of the bay, where they hoped to land, but when they came near it, the night was so dark they could not see to steer between the great rocks along the shore.

As the storm grew worse the waves rose higher and higher. Through the darkness the men could sometimes see a flash of white foam which showed where the waves were breaking over the rocks.

The wind and water swept them on, and now the giant stones rose close on every side. Again a great wave lifted the little vessel high upon its crest; every moment the men expected to be dashed against the cruel rocks. They grasped the sides of the boat and waited for the crash which would probably end life for them all.

Yet the boat was not dashed to pieces. When the wave rolled back into the sea it left the vessel upon a bit of sandy beach between the rocks. The moment the men felt the boat touch the sand they leaped out and pulled it high upon the shore out of reach of the waves.

The men gathered brushwood and, in the shelter of a great rock, built a roaring fire and camped for the night. Before they slept the Pilgrims knelt upon the ground and gave thanks to God for guiding them through the storm and darkness. Then they repeated a beautiful old song from the Bible beginning:

"O give thanks unto the Lord, for He is good, for His mercy endureth for ever."

The next morning the Pilgrims walked around the island, but they found no houses or people there. They climbed the hill to a great rock from which they could see all over the island. There were woods, ponds, and little streams, but no fields, nor any signs of life.

The island was not large enough to be a good place for their settlement. There would not be wood or game enough on it to last many years, and they needed more land for their farms.

The Pilgrims looked about for a tall, straight tree from which to make a new mast for their boat, and soon the chips were flying from a fine young cedar, as the men stripped off its branches and bark. When the new mast was in place and the rudder repaired, the boat was ready for another journey.

But the next day was Sunday, so the Pilgrims rested quietly on the island.

When Monday morning dawned the sea was still rough, but in the bay the water was smooth and blue. As they sailed slowly along near the shore, the Pilgrims sometimes stopped to measure the depth of the water. Here it was deep enough to float the largest ships.

One large rock lay at the edge of the water, and the men rowed the boat to it. They stepped out upon the rock and looked eagerly about them.

There was space enough on that sunny hillside for all their fields. At the foot of the hill flowed a brook of clear, sweet water.

After drinking from the brook the men walked up the hill to the woods. From the top of the hill they could see a long distance up and down the shore.

"If we build our village here, this high hill will be just the place for our fort," said Miles Standish.

The Pilgrims thought the matter over carefully, for there must be no mistake in choosing a place to settle.

There were a deep, safe harbor and plenty of running water. The earth seemed to be rich and free from stones and stumps. It looked as though the Indians had once raised corn here. Perhaps they had cleared the land.

Since the forest was at the top of the hill, it would not be hard to get logs for their houses. What better place could they find?

So the men sailed back to the *Mayflower* to tell the other Pilgrims the good news. How glad they were to know that a good place had been found for their homes!

"If I am not mistaken," said Governor Carver, "the little bay where we landed has been called Plymouth Bay."

The Pilgrims decided they would keep the name. It would remind them of the town of Plymouth in England, where many of them had friends.

The Pilgrims were eager to begin their houses at once, so the *Mayflower* sailed into the deep quiet waters of Plymouth Bay. When it was within a stone's throw of the shore, it could go no farther, and the smaller boat was made ready to carry them to the land.

The men were not the only ones to go. Several of the women wished to see the place that had been chosen for their home. So the boat carried Mistress Brewster, Mary Chilton, Mistress Carver, and a number of others besides the men.

They rowed up to the large rock by the shore. It was the only dry landing place on the beach, for the water was very shallow there.

As the boat reached the rock, and almost before it came to a standstill, out sprang Mary Chilton upon this famous stone, saying with a laugh, "I will be the first woman to step foot in our new town." And so she was.

The rock upon which she stepped is still near the ocean where it was when the Pilgrims came. It is called Plymouth Rock, and each year many go to the town of Plymouth and look at the place where the Pilgrims landed.

When all had landed, Mary Chilton, Priscilla, and the Allerton girls tripped along the beach, stopping now and then to pick up a shell or a pretty stone. As they came near a little thicket of trees hung with wild grapevines, Mary stopped to listen.

"I hear the sound of running water," she said. "There must be a spring near by." The girls all stood still and listened to the trickling water. It was like sweet music to their ears.

They hurried on and soon came to a rocky nook where the water bubbled and sang as it escaped from the dark earth.

Never had water tasted so good, the girls thought, as they dipped it up in their large shells. Not in all the years they lived in Holland had they tasted water fresh from a cold spring.

"Here are some wild plum and crab apple trees. What a beautiful spot this will be next May when these trees are in bloom!" exclaimed Remember Allerton. Then the girls tried to think how this bleak hillside would look next summer when it would be dotted with cottages, and the fields were green with growing corn.

"I am afraid there will not be any bright gardens such as we had in Leiden," said Priscilla, "for I doubt if there is a flower seed on the ship."

"Oh, yes, there is," answered Mary Chilton. "I thought about that last summer, and gathered ever so many seeds. Each of us can have a little flower bed. We will save the seeds again and by another year we will have enough to make the whole village bright with blossoms."

A sharp, cold sleet now began to fall, and summer and blossoms seemed far away. The women hurried back to the boat, but some of the men stayed to plan for the new town.

THE "MAYFLOWER."

The First Winter in Plymouth

The Pilgrims could hardly wait until morning to begin building the town. It was scarcely daylight when they loaded their axes, guns, saws, and hammers on the boat and rowed to shore.

"First we will build a large log house at the foot of the hill," said Governor Carver. "It will be strong and safe, and we can all live there while we are building our own houses."

While some measured the space for the common-house, others went to the forest to cut trees. You could hear their axes ring from morning till night. They had no horses to help them, and their hands must do all the work. So they dragged and rolled the logs from the forest.

John Howland called Giles Hopkins, Francis and John Billington, Love Brewster, and several others. "Come, boys," he said, "bring your sharp knives and we will go to the pond and cut rushes to thatch the roof."

William Bradford saw them start, and he shouldered his gun and went with them. If Indians should come, one man could not protect so many children. When they came to the pond, they cut the long rushes and tied them in bundles to carry back to the men. Once they heard the wild yell of Indians, and sometimes the howl of wolves in the forest, but they did not come near.

It was Christmas day when the first logs were cut and in three weeks the common-house was finished. It was a rough building, with its thatched roof and unplastered walls. The windows were made of oiled paper instead of glass. But it was their own, and the Pilgrims felt very happy when it was done.

They made a wide street from the shore to the top of the hill. It was named for their old home in Holland and is still called Leiden Street.

When the common-house was finished, the Pilgrims began to build their little cottages on each side of Leiden Street. There were nineteen families for which to provide. John Alden was to live with Captain Standish and help him build his house. Other men who were alone would live with those who had families.

The winter grew colder and more bitter. There were many days that were so stormy no work could be done on the houses. Food was scarce, and every day some of the men tramped through the deep snow in search of game. Often they returned nearly frozen, and with empty game bags.

The Pilgrims were often wet and cold, and they did not have proper food. Do you wonder that many of them became sick and died?

Rose Standish was the captain's young wife. Her sweet face and gentle, loving manner had made her very dear to the Pilgrims. If any were homesick and lonely, Rose seemed to know best how to cheer them. She was always planning little comforts or pleasure for others.

But Rose was not so strong and well as the others. Miles Standish sighed as he saw her grow more weak and pale every day. "My poor little Rose!" he said. "You are too frail a flower for this rough, wild life."

"I shall be better when I can leave the ship and breathe the sweet, fresh air of the earth and woods," she said.

So, as soon as the common-house was finished, Miles Standish gently lifted Rose into the smaller boat and took her to the shore. He carried her in his strong arms to the new log house and laid her upon a little cot.

The brave captain trembled with fear as he saw her flushed face and held her fevered hand. He knew an enemy had come that he could not conquer.

A few more days of suffering, and then Miles Standish was left alone.

Soon William Bradford became very ill, and then Goodman White, Mistress Allerton, and many others. In the common- house were long rows of white cots where lay suffering men and women.

At last there came a time when there were but seven well enough to hunt food, care for the sick, and bury the dead.

All day Priscilla moved quietly about, bathing fevered faces, or with cool hand rubbing the pain from some aching head. Or she bent over the coals of the fire making broth or toast for the sick, or cooking for those who nursed them.

At night when only a dim candle lighted the room, Doctor Fuller or Miles Standish went from bed to bed, giving a cool drink to one, or turning a heated pillow for another. Often a cup was placed in the hand of one of the weary nurses and Priscilla would whisper, "Drink this hot broth. It will give you strength to help others."

If it were their white-haired elder who was on watch, she would beg him to lie down and rest for an hour while she took his place.

"No, no, Priscilla," he would say, "you cannot work all day and watch at night. Take your rest, child, you need it much."

Then she would go back to her bed, stopping to smooth a pillow or speak a cheery word to someone too ill to sleep.

But even tender nursing could not bring health and life to all. Every day there was a new grave to be made on Cole's Hill.

At last came a morning when Priscilla could not rise. She was burning with fever and in her sleep talked of her old home in France. She thought she was a little girl playing with baby Joseph. She could not even understand when, one by one, her mother, father, and brother were laid under the snow on the hill.

The Pilgrims were afraid to have the Indians see so many graves. Perhaps they would attack the town if they knew there were so few of the white men left.

So late at night a little group of men carried their sad burden up the hill. When the grave was filled, they covered it over with snow so the Indians might not see it so easily.

In a few weeks half of the little band of Pilgrims lay buried on Cole's Hill. Those that remained alive found comfort in the fact that their departed friends had gone to be with the Lord.

Comprehension Exercises

Fill in the blanks

1. The Pilgrims first built a _____ to live in.

2. The children cut _____ from the pond.

3. The wide street they made is named _____ Street.

4. The winter was hard and _____ was one of the first to die.

5. Soon only _____ people were well enough to care for the   others.

6. In a few weeks time, _____ of the Pilgrims had died.

Samoset

At last spring came, bringing health and hope to the Pilgrims. Again the axes rang out in the forest, and the half-built cottages were soon finished. The snow melted from the sunny hillsides, and the ice in the streams broke away and floated into the sea.

One morning the men of Plymouth met in the common-house to make plans for their little army. "On the top of the hill we will build a large, strong fort, and mount our cannons upon it so they will point in every direction," said Captain Miles Standish. "If the Indians make trouble, we will bring the women and children to the fort for safety."

As he spoke there was a frightened scream from the children at play outside. The next moment a tall, half-naked Indian stood in the door before them.

Three eagle feathers were braided into his long black hair. Lines of red and black were painted upon his face. In his hand he carried a long bow and a quiver of arrows hung between his bare shoulders.

The Pilgrims sprang to their feet, seizing their guns and swords. Perhaps he was only one of many who were already in the village.

The Indian did not move from his place, though he laid his hand upon a little hatchet at his belt. How sharply his bright eyes glanced from one to another of the men!

"Welcome, Englishmen!" said he.

"What! Do these people speak English?" asked William Bradford.

"Look to your guns, men," said Captain Miles Standish in a low voice. "He may not be so friendly as he seems."

Perhaps the Indian understood the Captain's words, for he said quickly, "Samoset friend of Englishmen. He come to say welcome."

Elder Brewster stepped forward and gave his hand to the strange visitor. "Thank you for your kind words, friend. Where did you learn our language?"

"Samoset is chief in little land in the sea. Many English come there to fish and buy furs. Samoset much good to Englishmen."

"How far away is your island?" asked the elder.

"Come big wind in ship, one day. Or canoe to shore, then walk, five days," answered the chief.

"And which way did you come, Samoset?"

"Samoset come in ship eight moons ago. English friend give Samoset and other chiefs long ride in his ship."

Then the Pilgrims asked the Indian to sit down in the common-house with them. They brought him food and drink, and as he ate they asked him many questions.

"Are your Indian friends near here?" asked Captain Standish.

"Many Indians in forest," answered Samoset. "They bring many furs to trade with white men. Indians great hunters. White man not know how to make good traps like Indian."

The Pilgrims looked at William Bradford and smiled. He, too, was thinking of the Indian deer trap in which he had been caught one day.

"Samoset have Indian friend named Squanto. Him speak good English," said Samoset, as he took another leg of roast duck.

"Why did not Squanto come with you?" asked Elder Brewster.

"Squanto wise like fox. Him put his paw in trap one time. Him much afraid of white man now."

"Did the white men not treat him well?" asked Bradford.

Then Samoset laid down his bone and told them Squanto's story. He said, "Sailor-man tell Squanto to come have little ride in his white-winged canoe. Then he take Squanto and twenty other Indians to land of the sunrise, across the Big- sea-water. He sell them to be slaves.

"After many snows Squanto run away. Good fisherman bring him back home. He learn English in the white man's country."

Samoset did not seem in any hurry to leave the village. He walked about looking in at the doors or windows of the cottages. He knew the women and children were all afraid of him, and he seemed to enjoy their fright.

When night came he was still in the village. Some thought he was a spy sent to find out how strong the settlement was. They were afraid they would make him angry by sending him away.

"What shall we do with him?" they asked, as bedtime drew near.

"I believe he is a friendly Indian. He may stay in my house tonight," said Master Hopkins.

So Mistress Hopkins made a bed for him on a cot in the kitchen. But Samoset would not sleep on the cot. He spread a deerskin on the floor and slept before the fireplace. His dark skin glistened in the firelight as he slept.

But Master Hopkins did not sleep. All night long he lay and watched the Indian on his hearth. He dared not close his eyes for fear he would awake to find his family killed and his house in flames.

Very few of the Pilgrims slept well that night. If they heard an owl hoot or a wolf howl in the forest, they thought it was the yell of Indians come to destroy their town.

But the night passed in safety, and in the morning Samoset bade his new friends good-bye. The Pilgrims gave him some beads and an English coat which pleased him very much.

"Come again tomorrow and bring your friends," said William Bradford, as he walked with Samoset to the edge of the town. "Tell the Indians to bring their furs and we will pay for them, but you must not bring your bows and arrows, knives or hatchets into our settlement."

Comprehension Questions

1. What did they build on the hill?

2. Who came to visit the Pilgrims?

3. How did Samoset learn to speak English?

4. What had Squanto been?

5. Who did Samoset stay with that night?

6. What did William Bradford say to Samoset when he left?

The Treaty of Peace

The next day passed and no Indians came to the village. The day after this was Sunday, and the Pilgrims were always careful to make Sunday a holy day. They met in the common-house to sing and pray to God, and to listen to Elder Brewster's sermon.

When their service was over, they started quietly toward their homes. Before them marched Captain Standish with his gun, ready to give the alarm if he saw any danger.

Suddenly five great Indians came out of the forest. They wore suits of deerskin, and their faces were streaked with bright-colored paints. In their hair they wore long eagle feathers, and each man carried a roll of fine furs.

"It is Samoset and his friends. That means five more hungry men to feed," said Priscilla to Mistress Brewster.

"I think we have plenty of food to share with them," answered Mistress Brewster. "We will set the table for them in the common-house, and they need not come into our houses at all. It frightens the children to see them looking in at the doors."

After the Indians had eaten their dinner, they spread their furs upon the table. Then they motioned to bowls and kettles, and knives, and other things which they wanted in return for their rolls of furs.

"No, Samoset, this is Sunday. This is our Lord's Day. Tell your friends we cannot trade with them on the Lord's Day. Come tomorrow and we will be glad to buy your furs."

Samoset could not see why one day was any better than another, but he told his friends what the Pilgrims had said. So the Indians rolled up their furs and without another word walked out of the village.

Several days passed and the Indians did not return. The Pilgrims began to wonder if their visitors were angry because they had not taken the furs on Sunday.

The men were again in the common-house drawing plans for the fort to be built upon the hill, when Francis Billington and Love Brewster rushed into the room. They were pale with fright and out of breath with running.

"Indians! Indians!" they gasped. "We were down by the brook - gathering willows - to make whistles - and we saw - at least a hundred Indians - come out of the woods."

But Miles Standish did not wait to hear the end of their story. He ran to the door and looked toward the forest. Yes, the boys were right, there was a large band of Indians on the hill nearby. They talked together and pointed toward Plymouth village.

Quickly Captain Standish turned and gave his orders. Each man knew just where he was to stand and what he was to do in case of an attack.

Then Samoset and another Indian left the band and came slowly down into the village. Miles Standish and Edward Winslow went forward to meet them.

"This is Squanto, friend of English," said Samoset.

"You are both welcome to our village," answered Edward Winslow. "We hope you have brought many furs to trade with us today."

"No furs," replied Samoset. "Massasoit, the Great Chief of red men, comes to meet the White Chief. Massasoit would be the White Chief's brother."

When the Pilgrims learned that the king of many tribes waited to see them, they wished to show him honor. Governor Carver prepared some gifts for the chief, and Edward Winslow, wearing his finest armor, went with Squanto to the place where the Indians waited.

Massasoit looked like a king as he rested his long bow upon the ground and stood to receive the white man. He was very tall and straight. His garments of deerskin were beautifully trimmed with shells and shining quills, and he wore a band of eagle feathers which reached from the top of his head to the ground.

Upon the grass before Massasoit, Edward Winslow spread a red blanket of fine wool, upon which he placed strings of bright beads, a knife, and a long copper chain.

When he had slowly and carefully arranged all these things, Winslow arose and said to Massasoit, "My chief sends to you these gifts and invites you to his house. He would be your friend."

When Squanto had told Massasoit these words, the chief motioned Winslow to stay there until he returned. Then taking twenty of his warriors, he went to the village, led by Squanto.

Captain Standish, Master Allerton, and six other soldiers dressed in their bright armor met Massasoit and his men at the brook and escorted them to the common-house.

Here a large rug was spread and cushions were laid for the chief and his braves.

Soon the sound of drum and fife was heard, and Governor Carver entered, followed by the rest of the little army.

Then the meat and drink were brought, and, after the company had eaten together, Governor Carver and Massasoit made a treaty of peace.

Massasoit arose and in his own language promised that the Indians would not harm the white men, and if other Indian tribes made war upon Plymouth, Massasoit would help the Pilgrims.

He promised that his tribes should not bring their bows and arrows into the white men's settlement.

When Samoset had told in English what Massasoit had said, Governor Carver spoke. He said the Pilgrims would not harm the Indians, or carry their guns into the Indian villages when they went there to visit. He promised Massasoit they would always pay the Indians a fair price for the furs and other things they bought from them. When the governor's words had been told to Massasoit by Squanto, a treaty of peace was signed. The Indian chief could not write, but, instead, he made a little cross. Massasoit did not understand the signing of the paper. When Indians make a treaty of peace the two chiefs always smoke a peace pipe. So the governor and the chief smoked the great stone peace pipe which Samoset brought to them. "Now are the white men and the red men always brothers," said Samoset.

Then Massasoit unrolled the gifts he had brought to his white brother, Governor Carver. There were the finest of furs, a bow and arrows like his own, and a necklace of bears' teeth.

When Massasoit and his company were ready to return to their camp, Captain Standish and his soldiers escorted them as far as the brook, to show them honor.

This treaty of peace between the Pilgrims and the Indians was kept for fifty years. In all this time they did not break their promises to each other.

Squanto

When Massasoit and his people returned to their camp in the forest, Squanto did not go with them.

"Many, many moons ago wigwams of Squanto's people stand here, and here," he said, pointing to the shore and the brookside. "Many canoes on shore. Many camp fires on hillside."

"Did your tribe move to some other place, Squanto?" asked Elder Brewster.

"No," answered the Indian sadly. "Black sickness come. Papoose all die. Squaws all die. Chief and braves die. Only Squanto get well. Squanto come home now, and live with white brothers."

The Pilgrims were glad to have Squanto live with them, for he helped them in many ways. He knew every path in the forest and was their guide when they went there to hunt. He knew just where the deer went to drink, and in which streams to find the busy beavers.

He taught the Pilgrims how to make a trap near the spring where the deer came to drink. He bent down a strong branch of a tree and fastened it to the ground. When the deer stepped upon the end of the branch, it caught his foot and flew up, carrying the deer high in the air.

"This is a cruel trap, Squanto. We will never use it if we can get food any other way," said William Bradford.

"No, better to shoot deer," answered Squanto. "Poor Indian not have gun like white man."

He taught them how to make a snare of willow twigs and put it in the brook to catch fish. He knew how to make a bear trap of logs, and how to call the wild ducks and other birds.

Squanto could go through the forest without making a dry leaf rustle or breaking a twig. He could lie down on the ground and move through the tall grass without being seen.

When the Pilgrims and the Indians met to trade, Squanto could always tell each what the other said. "How could we ever talk to the Indians if Squanto should die?" thought Edward Winslow. "I think I will learn the Indian language while Squanto is here to teach me."

So the Indian became Winslow's patient teacher, and when these two were together they used the Indian language. This pleased Squanto very much, for English was hard for him.

The printed page was a great wonder to Squanto. He called it the "speaking paper." Indians sometimes wrote with paint upon a large flat rock, or with a bit of charcoal upon a piece of birch bark, but their writing was all in pictures.

Squanto was eager to learn to read the white man's books. "Teach Squanto to make paper talk," he said to Winslow one day.

Indian picture writing

So that evening when the candles were lighted, Squanto came to Master Winslow's house for his lesson. There were no primers or first readers in Plymouth then, but Winslow took down his Bible. It was the book from which he had learned to read; he would teach Squanto from it.

Every evening the Indian and his friend bent over the old book, spelling out its wonderful stories.

One day Squanto came in from the forest, carrying a little oak branch in his hand. Pointing to its tiny leaves, he said, "See! Oak leaves big like squirrel's foot. Time to plant corn now."

Then he went down to the brook and set a snare to catch the fish as they swam up the stream. The next morning Elder Brewster met Squanto coming from the brook with a large basket full of little fish.

"Why, Squanto!" he said. "What are you going to do with those tiny fish? They are too small to eat."

"Indians plant corn in these fields many times," answered Squanto. "Ground hungry now. We must feed the hungry earth." So he showed the Pilgrims how to put two little fishes into each hill of corn. They were glad to do as Squanto taught them, for they had never planted corn before.

Comprehension Questions

1. How did Squanto's people die?

2. What were some of the things Squanto taught the Pilgrims?

3. To whom did Squanto teach the Indian language?

4. What did Squanto call the Pilgrims' printed books?

5. Why did Squanto and the Pilgrims put fish into the hills as they planted corn?

Back to England?

One day, almost before the snow had melted from the ground, Priscilla, Mary Chilton, and some of the other girls began to look for spring flowers near the edge of the forest.

They brushed away the dry leaves to see if the violets or windflowers had started to grow. Sometimes they found, pushing their way up through the earth, a group of tiny rough balls which would some day unroll into a beautiful fern.

There were many pale little plants lifting their first buds up through the earth and leaves, but not a flower on any of them.

"It must be too early for blossoms," said Mary Chilton. "See, there are still patches of snow in that shady hollow."

"This is Mistress Brewster's birthday, and I did hope we could find a few blossoms for her," said Priscilla.

"Since she cannot come to the woods, let us take some of the woods to her," said Mary, digging up a handful of earth and leaves.

"Why do you take those dry leaves?" asked one of the girls.

Mary lifted the old leaves of the little plant she held, and showed the furry stems and buds of the hepatica. "They will open in a day or two if we put them in the sun, and

Mistress Brewster will enjoy watching them unfold," she said.

When the basket was filled with the dead-looking earth and leaves, it seemed like a strange birthday present for the dear old lady whom the girls often lovingly called "mother." But it was not many days until dozens of little furry stems lifted their dainty purple and white blossoms above the brown leaves.

As the girls came out of the forest, they looked across the water to where the *Mayflower* still lay in the harbor. The ship swung lightly to and fro as though glad to be free from the icy bounds which had held it so many weeks.

The spring storms were over now, and the *Mayflower* must soon return to England. Every evening for a week the Pilgrims had bent over their rough pine tables, writing letters for the *Mayflower* to carry to friends across the sea.

It was eight months since they had left England, and there was so much to write in these first letters to their friends. They must tell about the place where they had settled, the new homes they were making, and about their Indian neighbors.

Then there was the sad story of sickness and death, which must be told. Many of the letters were full of sadness and longing for England.

As the girls walked slowly down the hill each was thinking of all that had happened to the little band since the *Mayflower* dropped anchor in that harbor.

"There must be a meeting in the common-house this morning," said Mary Chilton, as she noticed a number of people entering the square log building. "Let us go in."

When they entered the large room, they saw the captain of the *Mayflower* standing before the people. He was thanking the Pilgrims for the kindness they had shown to him and to his men; for nursing them when they were ill, and for sharing their provisions with them when food was so scarce.

"Tomorrow, if the wind is fair, we set sail for England," he said. "You have had a sad, hard winter here. Many of those whom the *Mayflower* brought to this shore are dead. Now that there are so few of you, are you not afraid to stay here in this lonely land? If any of you wish to return to England, I will give you free passage."

The Pilgrims thought of the loved ones they had lost, and of the new grave on the hill where, only a few days before, they had laid their dear governor, John Carver.

Mistress Brewster's eyes grew dim as she thought of her son, and of Fear and Patience so far across the water. Should she return to them? "No," she thought, "we are making them a better home here, and sometime they will come to us."

William Bradford, who had been chosen as the new governor, was the first to speak.

"Men, you have heard the captain's offer. What do you say? Do any of you wish to return to England?"

"No," came the answer. "Our homes are here, and here we will stay."

"And these maids who have lost both father and mother, do they not wish to return to their old homes across the sea?" asked the ship's captain.

"Speak, Priscilla," said Governor Bradford.

"I have no home other than the one Elder Brewster and his wife so kindly offered me," said Priscilla.

"I have no wish to return, since all I have is here," said Mary Chilton.

Again Governor Bradford spoke. "Do not answer in haste," he said. "Think what it means to remain in this wild new land. Let each man answer for himself and his family. What say you, Master Allerton?"

"I and my family will stay," he replied.

So said all the others. Not one of the brave men and women accepted the captain's offer.

The First Thanksgiving

The summer days were full for the busy Pilgrims. In the fields there were only twenty men and a few boys to do all the work. There was corn to hoe, and there were gardens to weed and care for. When time could be spared from this work, there were barns to be built, and the fort to finish.

The brave men worked from morning till night preparing for the next long winter. The sun and the rain helped them. The crops grew wonderfully, and soon the hillsides were green with growing corn, and wheat, and vegetables.

When the warm days of early summer came, there were sweet wild strawberries on the sunny hills. A little later, groups of boys and girls filled their baskets with wild raspberries and juicy blackberries from the bushes on the edge of the forest. Sugar was too scarce to be used for jellies and preserves, but trays of the wild fruits were placed in the sun to dry for winter use.

The fresh green of the wheat fields began to turn a golden brown. The harvest was ripening. Before long the air rang with the steady beat of the flail, as the Pilgrims threshed their first crop of golden grain.

Soon the corn was ready to be cut and stacked in shocks. Then came the early frosts, and the Pilgrims hurried to gather the sweet wild grapes from vines which grew over bushes and low trees near the brook. The frost had opened the prickly burs and hard brown coats of the nuts, and every day Squanto went with a merry group of boys to gather chestnuts, hickory nuts, beechnuts, and walnuts.

At last the harvest was all gathered in. The Pilgrims rejoiced as they saw the bountiful supply of food for the winter. Some of the golden ears of corn they hung above the fireplace to dry for seed. The rest they shelled and buried in the ground, as Squanto showed them how to do.

As the evenings grew longer and cooler, the Pilgrims often went in to spend an hour or two at Elder Brewster's. The men piled great logs upon the fire. Then the girls and boys drew the chairs and benches nearer the huge fireplace, and all would set in the twilight and talk.

Sometimes they spoke of old times in England, or Holland, but usually it was of their work and the life in their new home. On this November evening everyone talked of the harvest which had just been stored away.

"Friends," said Governor Bradford, "God has blessed our summer's work, and has sent us a bountiful harvest. He brought us safe to this new home and protected us through the terrible winter. It is fit we have a time for giving thanks to God for His mercies to us. What say you? Shall we not have a week of feasting and of thanksgiving?"

"A week of thanksgiving!" said the Pilgrims. "Yes, let us rest from our work and spend the time in gladness and thanksgiving. God has been very good to us."

So it was decided that the next week should be set aside for the harvest feast of thanksgiving, and that their Indian friends should be asked to join them.

Early the next morning Squanto was sent to invite Massasoit with his brother and friends to come the following Thursday.

When he returned, a party of men took their guns and went into the woods for two days of hunting. They would need many deer and wild ducks to feed so large a company.

Far away in the forest they heard the sound of wild turkeys. They hurried on in that direction, but the sound seemed as far away as ever.

Squanto knew how to bring the turkeys nearer. He made a kind of whistle out of a reed. When he blew it, it sounded like the cry of a young turkey.

"Squanto blow. Turkeys come. Then Squanto shoot! Ugh!" said the Indian, as he showed the Pilgrims his whistle. When the men came back from their hunt they brought a bountiful supply of game. There were deer, rabbits, wild ducks, and four large turkeys.

The next few days were busy ones in Plymouth kitchens. There were the great brick ovens to heat, and bread to bake, and game to dress.

"Priscilla shall be chief cook," said Mistress Brewster. "No one can make such delicious dishes as she."

As soon as it was light on Wednesday morning, a roaring fire was built in the huge fireplace in Elder Brewster's kitchen. A great pile of red-hot coals was placed in the brick oven in the chimney.

Then Mary Chilton and Priscilla tied their aprons around them, tucked up their sleeves, and put white caps over their hair. Their hands fairly flew as they measured and sifted the flour, or rolled and cut cookies and tarts.

Over at another table Remember Allerton and Constance Hopkins washed and chopped dried fruits for pies and puddings. Out on the sunny doorstone Love Brewster and Francis Billington sat cracking nuts and picking out the plump kernels for the cakes Priscilla was making. What a merry place the big kitchen was!

When the oven was hot, the coals were drawn out, and the long baking pans were put in. Soon sweet, spicy odors filled the room, and on the long shelves were rows and rows of pies, tarts, and little nut cakes.

In the afternoon all of the girls and boys took their baskets or pails and went to the beach to dig clams. "Clams will make a delicious broth. We shall need hundreds of them," said Priscilla.

While they were gone, some of the men brought boards, hammers, and saws and built two long tables out-of-doors near the common-house. Here the men would eat, and a table would be spread in the elder's house for the women and children.

It was Thursday morning, and the Pilgrims were up early to prepare for the guests they had invited to the feast of thanksgiving. The air was mild and pleasant, and a soft purple haze lay upon field and wood.

"We could not have had a more beautiful day for our feast," thought Miles Standish, as he climbed the hill to fire the sunrise gun.

Just then wild yells and shouts told the astonished Pilgrims that their guests had arrived. Down the hill from the forest came Massasoit, his brother, and nearly a hundred of his friends, dressed in their finest skins, and in holiday paint and feathers.

The captain and a number of other men went out to welcome the Indians, and the women hurried to prepare breakfast for them.

Squanto and John Alden built a big fire near the brook, and soon the clam broth was simmering in the great kettle.

The roll of the drum called all to prayers, for the Pilgrims never began a day without asking God's blessing upon it. "The white men talk to the Great Spirit," Squanto explained to Chief Massasoit. "They thank Him for His good gifts." The Indians seemed to understand, and listened quietly to the prayers.

Then all sat down at the long tables. The women were soon busy passing great bowls of clam broth to each hungry guest. There were piles of brown bread and sweet cakes; there were dishes of turnips and boiled meat, and later, bowls of pudding made from Indian corn.

While they were eating, one of the Indians brought a great basket filled with popped corn and poured it out upon the table before Elder Brewster. The Pilgrims had never seen pop corn before. They filled a large bowl with this new dainty and set it on the children's table.

When breakfast was over, there was another service of thanksgiving, led by Elder Brewster. Then Governor Bradford took his friends to the grassy common where they would have games.

A number of little stakes were driven into the ground, and here several groups of Indians and Pilgrims played quoits, the Indians often throwing the greater number of rings over the stakes.

Then the Indians entertained their friends with some wonderful tests in running and jumping. After this Governor Bradford invited the Indians to sit down on the grass and watch the soldiers drill on the common.

The Indians sat down, not knowing what to expect next, for they had never before seen soldiers drill. Suddenly they heard the sound of trumpets, and the roll of drums. Down the hill marched the little army of only nineteen men, the flag of old England waving above their heads.

To right and to left they marched, in single file or by twos and threes, then at a word from the captain, fired their muskets into the air. The Indians were not expecting this, and some sprang to their feet in alarm. Again came the sharp reports of the muskets. Many of the Indians looked frightened. "Have the white men brought us here to destroy us?" they asked.

"The white men are our friends; they will not harm us," answered Massasoit.

Hardly had he finished speaking when there came a deep roar from the cannon on the fort. The sound rolled from hill to hill. At this the Indians became more and more uneasy. They did not enjoy the way the white men entertained their guests.

Some thought of an excuse to leave the village. "We will go into the forest and hunt," they said. "We will bring deer for the white men's feast."

Captain Standish smiled as he saw the Indians start for the forest. "They do not like the thunder of our cannon," he said.

But the next morning the five Indians returned, each bringing a fine deer.

Saturday was the last day of the feast. How busy the women were preparing this greatest dinner! Of course the men and boys helped too. They dressed the game, brought water from the brook, and wood for the fire.

There were turkeys, stuffed with beechnuts, browning before the fire. There were roasts of all kinds, and a wonderful stew made of birds and other game.

And you should have seen the great dishes of purple grapes, the nuts, and the steaming puddings. The table seemed to groan under its load of good things. The Indians had never seen such a feast. "Ugh!" said Massasoit, as he ate the puffy dumplings in Priscilla's stew. "Ugh! The Great Spirit loves his white children best!"

So the happy day ended, and the Indians returned to their wigwams. The Pilgrims never forgot their first Thanksgiving day. Each year when the harvests were gathered, they would set aside a day for thanking God for

His good gifts, and for years their Indian friends joined in this feast.

"The Indians had never seen such a feast"

Comprehension Questions

1. Why did the Pilgrims have to work hard during the summer?

2. What kinds of food did they grow and gather for the winter?

3. Who suggested the idea of a week of thanksgiving?

4. What did Squanto explain to Chief Massasoit about the prayer time of the Pilgrims?

5. List some of the food that was prepared for this special time.

Thanksgiving

"Have you cut the wheat in the blowing fields,
The barley, the oats, and the rye,
The golden corn and the pearly rice?
For the winter days are nigh."

"We have reaped them all from shore to shore,
And the grain is safe on the threshing floor."

"Have you gathered the berries from the vine,
And the fruit from the orchard trees?
The dew and the scent from the roses and thyme,
In the hive of the honeybees?"

"The peach and the plum and the apple are ours,
And the honeycomb from the scented flowers."

"The wealth of the snowy cotton field
And the gift of the sugar cane,
The savory herb and the nourishing root-
There has nothing been given in vain."

"We have gathered the harvest from shore to shore,
And the measure is full and brimming o'er."

"Then lift up the head with a song!
And lift up the hand with a gift!
To the ancient Giver of all,
The spirit in gratitude lift!

For the joy and the promise of spring,
For the hay and the clover sweet,
The barley, the rye, and the oats,
The rice, and the corn, and the wheat,
The cotton, and sugar, and fruit,
The flowers and the fine honeycomb,
The country so fair and so free,
The blessings and glory of home."

Amelia E. Barr

Friends or Foes?

One day late in November, Governor Bradford and his friend Edward Winslow walked along the top of the hill toward Plymouth. They carried guns on their shoulders and their game bags were heavy with the wild ducks they were bringing home.

Suddenly they heard a light, quick step on the dry leaves behind them. They turned and saw an Indian running toward them. He pointed to the sea and tried to tell them something, but the Englishmen could not understand his language.

The three men hurried to the village, and Squanto was called to the common-house. To him the Indian told his message.

"He says a large ship is coming," said Squanto. "It is not far away. He thinks it is a French ship."

Governor Bradford looked sorely troubled. The French were not friendly with the English. If their ship came to Plymouth it would try to capture the town. The governor thanked the Indian for coming to warn him of the danger, and gave him presents and food.

Soon everyone in the town knew the word which the Indian had brought. Governor Bradford ordered a cannon to be fired to call home any who were away hunting or fishing.

Nearly everyone came down to the shore to watch for the ship. They had not waited long when a sail appeared around the point. Yes, it was coming straight toward Plymouth harbor.

Captain Miles Standish and some of the other men hurried to the cannon on the hill. They carefully aimed them at the coming vessel.

"If it is the ship of an enemy, we will be ready for it," said the captain. Every man, and every boy who was big enough, carried a gun.

As the boat drew nearer, the people became more and more excited. Hardly a word was spoken, but their white faces showed how anxious they were.

They shaded their eyes with their hands and tried to see what flag floated from its mast. In every heart was a prayer that it might be that of old England.

Nearer and nearer came the ship. All eyes were fixed upon the masthead. Now a flash of white could be seen, but what were the darker colors? Breathless they waited. As the flag again fluttered in the breeze, a bright red cross flashed into sight.

"The flag of old England!" "It is an English ship!" "An English ship!" The hills rang with their joyful shouts.

From the cannon on the fort a roar of welcome boomed across the water, and a minute later came an answer from the cannon on the ship.

Priscilla darted away up the hill to the elder's cottage, where Mistress Brewster, too weak to leave the house, sat waiting at the window. One glance at Priscilla's sunny face told her the ship was from England.

"Oh, Mother, dear, it is an English ship. Perhaps Patience and Fear, or Jonathan is upon it," cried Priscilla. "Sit close to the window, and I will run home and tell you when I see them." Leaving Mistress Brewster with her face buried in her trembling hands, the girl hurried back to the shore. There the children who had been silent with fright now shouted and ran up and down the beach. They could hardly wait for the ship to land.

"I hope my brother Jonathan is on that boat," said Love Brewster, hopping first on one foot and then on the other.

"So do I," cried one of the others.

"I wish it would bring some more little children to play with. You big boys never let me play with you," said little Samuel.

"That is because you can't run fast enough, Samuel. You would get lost. What do you wish for, Francis Billington?"

"I wish it would bring me a soldier suit and a sword like the captain's 'Gideon,'" said Francis. This was a wild wish indeed. Who ever heard of a little boy having a soldier suit and a sword!

Giles Hopkins would not waste his wish on anything which he knew could not come true.

"I wish it would bring the cow we left in England. I am so hungry for some milk, and butter, and cheese. I am just tired of beans, and bread with no butter."

"Be glad you have the beans and bread, Giles," said Priscilla, coming up behind them. "Elder Brewster says there is hardly enough corn to last through the winter, and the other grain is nearly gone. We had better wish the English ship would bring us more meal."

Just then a small boat was lowered from the side of the ship. All watched to see the men climb down the rope ladder into it, though they could not see who they were at this distance.

Some of the Pilgrims were expecting brothers, some were looking for sons or daughters, others for friends. It seemed to those on shore that the men rowed very slowly.

But at last the little boat touched the stone which we call Plymouth Rock. Almost the first to leap ashore was Elder Brewster's oldest son. Little Love had his "wish." There were other dear old friends who had been left in England or Holland, and there were some people whom the

Pilgrims did not know, about thirty-five in all. How glad the Pilgrims were to see them!

When the captain of the vessel came ashore, he brought a large bag of mail. It was now just a year since the *Mayflower* had brought the little band of Pilgrims to this new land. In all this time they had not heard one word from their friends at home. Now there were letters for all.

The candles burned late in Plymouth that night. In Elder Brewster's home the last candle had flickered and gone out, but still the family sat about the blazing fire and listened while Jonathan told them of Fear and Patience, and of many old friends in Holland.

The ship had not brought the provisions that the Pilgrims so much needed. It had not even brought food for its passengers. There had been hardly enough for the voyage, and the Pilgrims must give the sailors food for the trip back to England.

After that, they would have barely corn enough for themselves during the long winter; yet here were thirty-five more hungry mouths to be fed. What had been a bountiful supply of food for fifty was a very small amount for eighty-five.

But the corn, and the barley, and the dried fruits, and smoked fish were equally divided among them. They must all have been hungry many times, but none died for lack of food.

The Pilgrims tried to buy corn from the Indians who lived near by, but they had none to spare. The snow was so deep and the ice so thick that hunting and fishing were almost impossible.

Winter 1621 — Spring 1622

Winter dragged slowly. The food was nearly gone. Something must be done very soon. So Governor Bradford and a few others rowed away to buy food from a tribe of Indians who lived a long way from Plymouth. They were gone many days, but when they returned their boat was well loaded with baskets of corn.

At last spring came. The streams were full of fish. Deer, wild turkeys, and other game could be found in the forest, and there was food enough for all.

It was not long before many new cabins were built along Leiden Street, and other streets were being made. Scores of new farms were cleared that summer, and soon the sunny hillsides rocked with the waving grain.

During the spring and summer several other ships came, bringing hundreds of passengers. These people did not all settle at Plymouth. They made homes for themselves and formed new towns, or settlements, a few miles away.

At last the smoke went curling up from many chimneys in New England, as this part of our country is still called. One of these towns was Boston, another was Salem, and there were many others. They were all very friendly with one another, and the people were never again so sad or lonely as the Pilgrims had been.

Comprehension Questions

1. Why were the Pilgrims worried about the Indian's report of seeing a ship?

2. What were some of the wishes of the children?

3. How many people came on this trip?

4. What happened during the next spring and summer?

5. What were the names of two of the new towns?

Tit for Tat

"Do any of you know where Squanto is?" asked Miles Standish, coming into the common-house where Governor Bradford and Edward Winslow sat writing. "I can see an Indian running down the beach toward the town; I suppose he is a messenger."

"Squanto has gone to the forest to hunt deer, and will not be home until night," answered the governor. "Bring the Indian here and perhaps Winslow can understand his message."

So Miles Standish left the room, and soon returned with the Indian, who carried in his hand a bundle of arrows wrapped with the skin of a large snake.

The Indian did not return the governor's friendly greeting. Throwing the bundle of arrows upon the table, with an ugly rattle, he gave them his message. But Governor Bradford and Miles Standish did not know what he said, and Edward Winslow could understand a word only now and then.

When the Indian had finished speaking, he turned to leave the village, but Governor Bradford would not let him go. "You must wait until Squanto comes to tell us your message," Winslow explained to him.

Captain Standish was given charge of the Indian, and he took his unwilling guest home to dinner. But the messenger had heard wonderful tales about the "Thunder

Chief," as the Indians called Captain Standish. Many of the Indians believed he had the deadly black sickness buried under his cabin and could send it upon his enemies if he wished. The Indian was too frightened to eat, and insisted upon returning to his people.

"He . . . filled the snake skin with powder and shot"

Night came, and Squanto had not returned. Governor Bradford came over to the captain's cottage and found the Indian walking angrily up and down the room.

"It is not right to hold a messenger against his wish," said the governor. "We will have to let him go." So the Indian was set free and he quickly sped out of the town.

The next morning when Squanto returned, the snake skin of arrows was shown to him. "What do you understand these arrows to mean?" asked the captain.

Squanto's eyes flashed with anger. "Arrows say, 'Come out and fight.' Soon many arrows fly in this village. Many white men die."

"Our bullets fly farther than arrows. We are not afraid," answered Bradford. He threw the arrows upon the ground and filled the snake skin with powder and shot. Handing it to Squanto, he said, "Take that to the chief. Tell him we have done him no harm, but we are ready to fight if he comes."

Two days later Squanto reached the village of the chief who had sent the arrows. These Indians did not have Massasoit as their king. They had never been friends with the white man. From a safe hiding place they had seen the second ship land its company of Englishmen upon their shores. "We will make war upon them, and kill them all now while they are so few," said their chief.

Squanto went at once to the wigwam of the chief. "The white men send you their thunder and lightning," he said, handing the chief the glistening snake skin.

The Indians had heard of the deadly weapon of the white man. A few of them had even heard its thunder, but none of them had ever touched a gun or seen powder and shot.

The Indians crowded around to see the strange bundle, but not one of them would touch it. The chief would not have it in his wigwam a minute. He ordered Squanto to take it back to Plymouth, but he would not. "There is plenty more there," said Squanto. "When you come you shall have it." Then he turned and left the village.

The chief then called another messenger and told him to take the hated bundle away, anywhere out of his country. So the messenger carried it to another tribe, but they would have none of it. It was passed from one Indian village to another, leaving terror in its path. At last, after many weeks, the snake skin of powder returned unopened to Plymouth.

That was all the Pilgrims ever heard of war with those Indians. But they thought it wise to protect their town better, so a high fence of pointed posts was built all around the town. For many weeks a watchman was kept at the gate night and day.

Comprehension Questions

1. What did the Indian messenger bring?

2. What did Squanto say the arrow and snake skin meant?

3. Did the angry Indians like what Squanto brought them? Why?

4. What did the Indians do with the skin sent by the Pilgrims?

5. What did the Pilgrims build to keep the town safer?

A PILGRIM FATHER IN HIS ARMOR.

Massasoit and the Medicine Men

One cold March day another Indian messenger appeared at the gate of Plymouth. He had been running many miles, and his body was wet and his veins were swollen.

"English friends come quick!" he cried. "Chief Massasoit much sick! Soon die!"

This was sad news to the Pilgrims, for Massasoit was their best friend among the Indians.

It was decided that Edward Winslow should be one of those to go with the messenger, for he was a good nurse, and he knew something of the Indian language.

The messenger was in too great a hurry to eat the food they gave him. He could hardly wait for Edward Winslow to prepare the medicines and food he wished to take Massasoit. "Great chief die soon!" he moaned. "Not see, not eat, for four days."

Soon the basket was ready and Winslow and another Englishman followed the guide into the forest. Faster and faster went the Indian, until the men could hardly keep up. Often the guide was so far ahead that he was almost lost to sight.

He must have thought that the Englishmen were very slow. He feared that Massasoit would die before they reached the village.

Indians do not usually say much about their joys or
sorrows, but Edward Winslow has told us how deeply this
guide grieved for his beloved chief. Often he would cry in
his own language, "Oh, my chief! My loving chief! I have
known many brave warriors, but none so brave, so kind,
so just as Massasoit!"

Sometimes he would say, "Oh, Master Winslow, what
friend will your people have among the Indians when
Massasoit is gone?"

On and on they hurried, hardly stopping to eat or rest. It
was now two days since they left Plymouth. The sun had
gone down in a bank of clouds, and already the shadows
were black and deep in the forest.

The wind whistled through the tree tops, and soon a fine,
sharp sleet began to fall. It was a bad night to be in the
woods, but the guide told them that the village was not far
off.

Above the voice of the storm came a distant moaning. At
first Winslow thought it was the sound of a great
waterfall.

"It sounds more like owls, or the cry of some animal," said
his companion.

But the guide knew the sound came from the wigwam of
Massasoit, and again he moaned, "Oh, my chief! My
chief!"

Now and then a gleam of light could be seen among the trees. Presently, in a little clearing, they came upon the Indian village. A great camp fire threw its unsteady light upon the wigwams in the village.

The lodge of Massasoit was larger than the others. There were pictures painted upon its sides, telling of the great deeds of Massasoit and his people.

Before the door of the wigwam hung a curtain of fine fur. Winslow pushed aside the curtain, but the room was so full of visitors that he could hardly enter.

The poor old chief lay on his cot. His eyes were closed. He could no longer see the friends about him. "He is dying," said an Indian who stood near, rubbing the chief's cold hands.

In a circle about the cot were five or six Indian medicine men. Their half-naked bodies were painted in many colors; upon their heads they wore the horns and skins of beasts. They danced around the chief, leaping, yelling, and waving their arms to frighten the sickness away.

Poor Massasoit! No wonder he was dying.

When the Indians saw the white men, they told Massasoit that his English friends had come to help him. The great chief loved Winslow, and put out his hand to welcome him.

"Your friends at Plymouth are all grieved to hear of your illness," said Edward Winslow, in the Indian language.

"Our governor has sent you some things which will help to make you well."

But Massasoit only shook his head. He did not think he could get well. His mouth and throat were so sore he could scarcely swallow, so he had eaten nothing for days.

Winslow opened his basket and took out two little jars of food which he had brought, the Indians crowding around to see. But, alas, the bottle of medicine he needed was broken. There was not a drop left.

He mixed the food with a little warm water and put some of it into the chief's mouth. Massasoit seemed to enjoy the dainty food which Winslow fed him, and whispered, "More."

The Indians had not forgotten the broth they had at the Feast of Thanksgiving. "Massasoit will get better if you give him white-man's broth," said one of them.

Only Priscilla knew what was needed to make and flavor that soup. There was nothing here from which to make it, even if Winslow had known how.

So he wrote a note asking Doctor Fuller to send such medicine as Massasoit needed, and, also, a pair of chickens and whatever else was necessary to make a good broth. A fresh messenger sped swiftly toward Plymouth with the note.

There was no fresh meat in the lodge, but Winslow must make a broth of some kind. In a large earthen bowl he saw some corn. He asked one of the squaws to pound it into meal, and when this had been done he made a thin soup of it.

In the woods near the wigwam he found some sweet roots and some fresh, young strawberry leaves. When he had flavored the soup with these, it was very good, and the chief drank it eagerly. He was getting better. He was soon so much better that he was able to see again.

Then Winslow bathed his face and hands, gave him a drink of cool water, and bade the Indians go away and leave him in quiet.

This was just what Massasoit needed, and he soon fell asleep. When the messenger returned, the chief was so much better that he did not need the medicine.

Of course Massasoit now loved the English more than ever. He told all his friends what had been done for him. After that many Indians came to Plymouth to get help for their sick friends.

The Englishmen taught them to make broth. They taught them that good food, fresh air, and pure water would help them more than all the noise and dances of medicine men.

Comprehension Questions

1. Who went to see if he could help Massasoit?

2. How do we know that the Indian messenger was very concerned for his chief?

3. How were the Indians trying to help their chief?

4. What did Winslow do for the chief?

5. What did the Englishmen teach the Indians to do for their sick people?

Troubles with the Indians

Many years had passed since the colonists first landed in New England. All this time they had lived at peace with the Indians. The Indians often came to the villages to trade with the settlers. They came to their houses, and many of them learned to speak a little English.

But the Indians were not all so friendly as Samoset, Squanto, and Massasoit. Many of them hated the white men and would have killed them if they had dared.

"See their cattle in our meadows," they said.

"They cut down our forests, and the deer no longer feed here," said others.

"They are not your forests and fields now," said Massasoit. "You sold them to the white men."

The Indians did not care for money. It was not pretty. They liked bright beads and shining buttons better. They liked English knives and red blankets.

But after a while the beads were lost and the blankets were worn out. The land which they had given for them did not wear out or get lost. The Indians looked at the rich farms; then they looked at their broken knives and ragged blankets.

"The palefaces have cheated us," they cried to their chief. "Let us make war upon them. Let us drive them from our land."

But Massasoit never forgot the promise he had made the white men so long ago. "They are our brothers," he said. "We will not harm them. Have you forgotten how they came to my lodge when I might have died? They have made schools for you; they have cared for you when you were sick. They have paid you what you asked for your land. They have kept their promise to us. We will keep our promise to them."

So as long as good Massasoit lived, the Indians made the Pilgrims no trouble. He was a great chief and many tribes obeyed him.

But at last a sad day came when Massasoit lay still in his wigwam. His friends, the Englishmen, stood around him, but they could not help him now. The great chief was dead.

After Massasoit's death his oldest son became chief. He was not very friendly toward the settlers.

It was nearly fifty years since the Pilgrims had founded Plymouth. In that time thousands of Englishmen had come to New England, and there were also colonists from France, Holland, and other countries.

Most of these people had come to gain wealth. They wanted the lands the Indians owned, and often fought for them instead of paying for them. Often they were unjust and in many ways very cruel to the Indians.

One day the new chief went to Plymouth to talk the matter over with his father's old friends. While he was there he became very ill. The colonists took good care of him and tried to make him well, but in a few days he died.

After his death his younger brother, Philip, became chief. He hated all settlers and wished to be rid of them. He believed they had killed his brother at Plymouth, and this made him hate them all the more.

So he sent word to many other tribes, saying that he was going to make war upon the settlers and asking them to join him. "We are stronger than the settlers, now," said he, "and if we all join in this war we can easily kill or drive them all out of the country."

Swift Indian runners carried the message to the chiefs of other tribes. But they had seen how cruelly the white men punished the Indians who tried to harm them, and were afraid.

One band of Indians had tried to kill the people of a little town not far from Plymouth, and the white men had destroyed the whole tribe. So the chiefs of the other tribes told Philip they would not join his war.

But Philip believed that his tribes alone were strong enough to drive out the colonists, and a terrible war was begun which we call King Philip's War.

The Indians never came out in open battle to fight like soldiers. They usually hid in the forest near some village until night, when the people were quietly sleeping; then, with terrible whoops and yells, they swept down upon it, burning the houses and killing as many people as they could.

Near King Philip's home was the little village of Swansea, and the chief decided this should be the first town to be destroyed. From their hiding place in the forest the Indians watched for a good chance to make the attack.

One Sunday morning, when all the people of Swansea were at church, Philip said, "This is a good time to get rid of these people. We will kill them all at once, when they come out of the meetinghouse."

When the service was over, the people came out never dreaming of the dreadful trouble awaiting them. Suddenly the air rang with the yells of the savages, and King Philip and his followers fell upon them.

When the sun set that day, the pretty village was in ashes and the streets were strewn with the dead and dying.

Sometimes a small band of Indians went into the country where there were little farms far from any town. They watched a cabin until they saw the men of the family go into the field to work; then, slipping up to the house, they would kill or steal the women and children, and set fire to the cottage.

But the Indians did not always succeed in their cruel work of destroying homes. Many lives and many homes were saved by the quick wits and the brave hearts of the boys and girls as well as of the older people.

In the following pages we will read about the experiences of some of the children in those early days so full of danger.

Comprehension Questions

1. Why were the fields and forests no longer the property of the Indians?

2. Why did the Indians think the Englishmen had cheated them?

3. Why did Massasoit say the Indians should keep their promises?

4. What were the names of Massasoit's sons?

5. What was the name of the war against the Pilgrims?

6. What was the name of the village King Philip attacked?

The Indians and the Lanterns

On a little farm several miles from any village, lived two little girls, Prudence and Endurance.

There were no other children near, but they were never lonely, for they had Whitefoot and Fluff, two of the prettiest kittens you ever saw. They had old Speckle and her little brood of downy, yellow chicks. Down in the pasture was Bess, the cow, with her pretty black and white calf. This was the greatest pet of all.

A tribe of Indians lived in the forest not far away. At first the children were very much afraid of them, but the Indians seemed friendly and made many visits to the house in the clearing.

Sometimes they came to trade their furs for a kettle, a blanket, or something else which they could not make.

Once a squaw came to bring her papoose, who was very ill. She wanted the white woman to make it well. The kind mother cared for the Indian baby as tenderly as though it were her own. Presently the little one was much better and went to sleep in its little cradle.

The Indian woman was very thankful. She gave Prudence a pretty little pocket trimmed with beads. Then she hung the papoose, cradle and all, upon her back and went home to her wigwam, feeling very happy.

One October day, their father said to Prudence and Endurance, "Children, mother and I must go to the village today. I think we shall be home before dark, but if we should have to stay away all night, do you think you are big enough and brave enough to keep house while we are gone?"

"Oh, yes," answered the children. "We shall not be afraid, and we shall be too busy to be lonely."

"There are a few more pumpkins in the field; you may roll them in and pile them with the others beside the pit I have dug for the potatoes," said their father. "If you wish, you may have two of the pumpkins for lanterns."

"We shall try to be back before dark, but if we are not here, just bolt the doors and you will be all right," said the mother, as she kissed the little girls good-bye. "Don't forget to cover the fire with ashes before you go to bed," she called, as she rode away.

The children watched their parents until a turn in the road hid them from sight; then they went in to finish the morning work. How grand they felt to be real housekeepers!

Endurance took down a turkey wing from its nail in the chimney corner, and brushed the hearth until not a speck of dust was left upon it. Then the girls swept and dusted the big kitchen, which was also the sitting room.

When it was time to get dinner, Endurance peeled some potatoes, and Prudence put more wood on the fire and hung a kettle of water over it for the tea. In another kettle she made a fine stew of meat and potatoes.

It seemed rather strange to sit down at the dinner table without Father and Mother, but after all it was great fun, for Prudence sat in mother's chair and poured the tea, while Endurance served the stew. In a chair between them sat Betty, the big rag doll, but she did not seem to be as hungry as the little housewives.

After the dishes were washed the children scampered to the field close by, and began to roll in the big orange pumpkins.

Late that afternoon their work was all done, and they sat down behind the great golden pile and began to make their lanterns. At last they were finished.

"Now I will go in and find some candle ends, and we will light our lanterns as soon as it is dark," said Endurance.

When she was gone, Prudence brought an armful of straw, and jumping into the pit, began to cover the earth with it. Her father would be surprised to find the potato pit so nicely lined with clean straw when he came home.

While she was at work, Prudence heard voices near the barn. "Oh, Father and Mother have come! I am so glad they did not stay all night," thought the child, climbing out of the pit to run to meet them.

But what changed her happy smile to a look of terror? What made her fall back upon the straw and cover her face with her hands? It was not Dobbin and the wagon she had seen at the barn door, but two Indians. One glance at their fierce, painted faces told her they were on the warpath.

For a few minutes she dared not move for fear the Indians would hear her. She expected every moment to be dragged from her hiding place.

Then she thought of her sister. What if Endurance should come out of the house and be seen by the Indians! At this terrible thought she sprang up and peeped out of the pit.

At first she could see nothing of the Indians, but soon they came out of the barn, carrying some pieces of harness and a new ax. They talked in a low tone and pointed toward the house, then disappeared behind the barn.

When they were gone, Prudence ran into the house, crying, "Oh, Endurance! Endurance! What shall we do? The Indians! Indians!"

"Well, they will not hurt us," said Endurance, "They often come here."

"But these are not our Indians. They belong to another tribe, and they are on the warpath. Oh, such terrible Indians! I am sure they will come back tonight and burn the house and kill or steal us."

But they were brave little girls and did not waste much time crying over this trouble. They began to plan what to do. "Let us light our lanterns and hide in the potato pit," said Endurance. "When they come we will hold up our lanterns and frighten them. Mother says Indians are very much afraid of things they cannot understand."

As soon as it was dark, the little girls lighted their lanterns and crept into the pit. They pulled some boards and brush over the hole and waited. It seemed to them they had waited hours and hours, when they heard soft footsteps coming toward the house.

The girls watched. In the darkness they could see two Indians creeping nearer and nearer, until they were quite close to the pit.

"Now!" whispered Endurance, and they pushed their lanterns up through the brush.

The Indians were so astonished that, for a moment, they stood perfectly still, staring at the lanterns. Then, with a yell of terror, they dropped their tomahawks and ran into the forest as fast as they could go.

All night long the girls lay in the pit. When morning came, they crept out and looked about. No Indians were to be seen. Beside the pit lay the tomahawks and, a little farther away, three eagle feathers, which one of the savages had dropped as he ran.

When their father and mother returned, the children told the story of the Indians and the lanterns, and showed the feathers and tomahawks.

"My brave, brave little girls!" whispered their father, as he held them close in his arms.

The Indians must have told their friends about the dreadful sight they had seen, for never after would an Indian go near that house.

"Ugh! Ugh! Fire spirits! Me 'fraid! Fire spirits!" they would say.

Comprehension Questions

1. What were the names of the two girls?

2. Where were the girls' mother and father going on their trip?

3. What were some of the things the girls did while their parents were gone?

4. Why was Prudence upset when she saw the two Indians?

5. Where were the girls hiding and how did they scare the Indians?

6. What did the Indians say they were afraid of near the house?

Indian cutting birch bark for a canoe

Two Little Captives

On a sunny hillside, near the river, a boy was cutting corn. It was late in September, but the day was warm. "This is just the day for a row on the river," said Isaac Bradley to himself.

As he looked over the bright, smoothly-flowing water, he saw a little boat coming toward him. In it, as the boat neared the shore, he saw his friend Joseph, who lived in the village of Haverhill a mile farther down the river.

Joseph tied his boat to the root of a tree on the bank, and came up into the field.

"Get your line and let's go fishing," he cried, as he climbed the hill.

"I cannot go until I finish cutting this corn," answered Isaac. "There are only a few rows more."

"Give me a knife and I will help you," said Joseph.

So he took one of the strong, sharp, corn knives and began to cut the dry stalks near the ground. In those days no one had thought of making a corncutter that could be pulled by a tractor.

Cutting corn with a knife was slow, hard work.

When they reached the end of the row, the boys stopped to rest. How warm and tired they were!

They were on the top of the hill now, near the edge of the woods. The forest once came almost down to the river. It had taken Mr. Bradley, and his father also, many years to clear the trees off this field.

The boys sat down in the shade of a tree to talk about their plans for the afternoon. Presently Joseph said, "Let us get a good, cool drink from the spring, and then finish cutting that corn."

Near the edge of the forest a spring of clear, cold water bubbled up out of the rocks. A tiny steam flowed from the spring and danced merrily down the hillside to join the broad river.

Joseph and Isaac knelt on the mossy rocks to drink. Suddenly two painted Indian warriors sprang from behind the bushes and seized the boys.

The frightened boys gave a loud, wild scream for help, but the rough hands of the warriors quickly covered their mouths, hushing their cries.

Mr. Bradley was at work at the other end of the field. He heard the scream and hurried to the spring, but the boys were not to be found. In the soft earth around the spring he saw the prints of Indian moccasins.

Meanwhile the boys were being hurried deeper and deeper into the forest. On and on they went, wading streams and climbing rocky hillsides. The thick branches tore their clothes and scratched their skin. At last they were so tired they could hardly walk.

The Indians allowed them to rest a little while, then on they went again. Now the sun had set, and it was almost dark in the forest. Soon they came to a hollow between two steep hills. Beside a little camp fire sat two more Indians. Several ponies were tied to the trees close by.

"Joseph and Isaac knelt on the mossy rocks to drink"

The Indians unbound their captives and motioned to them to sit down by the fire and then they began to cook a supper of deer meat. They gave the boys a handful of parched corn and some of the meat.

After the supper was eaten, all but one of the Indians lay down near the fire to sleep, making signs for Joseph and Isaac to sleep too.

Poor boys! How could they sleep with those fierce warriors beside them? The great, dark forest was all around them, and they were many miles from home and parents.

Joseph lay on his blanket and cried bitterly. Isaac, who was four years older, tried to comfort him.

"Don't cry, Joseph," he whispered. "I am sure father and other men from Haverhill will soon find us. No doubt they are on our trail this very minute. I would not be surprised if they came before morning."

"They can't find us," sobbed Joseph. "They do not know which way we have gone."

"The dogs will know. They can easily find the way," answered Isaac, cheerfully.

The next morning as soon as it began to be light, the Indians awoke. They placed the boys upon ponies, and, quickly mounting their own, led the way through the forest. All day they rode, stopping only two or three times to eat and rest.

Although Joseph was but eight years old, he was almost as large as Isaac; but he was not so strong, nor so brave-hearted. Every time they stopped to get a drink, or to rest, Joseph was sure the Indians intended to kill them.

"If they had intended to kill us, they would have done it before now," said Isaac. "I think they mean to take us to their camp and make us work for them. Or perhaps they mean to sell us to the French, but we can get away from them before that."

"Perhaps our fathers and the soldiers from the fort will come and get us," said Joseph, more cheerfully.

Just before night they came in sight of a large, beautiful lake. The water glowed with the soft colors of the sunset. Around the lake were great, dark pine trees, and maples with leaves as bright as flame.

Suddenly the boys saw the light of a camp fire shining through the trees. Then the whole camp could be plainly seen. It seemed to the frightened boys that there were dozens of wigwams in the village.

As they came nearer, they saw the dark forms of Indians moving around the fire. An Indian woman was roasting a large piece of meat on a forked stick.

When the Indians rode into the camp with their captives, the people all crowded around to see them. They smiled when they saw the boys' white, frightened faces.

The little Indians looked at them with wide, wondering eyes. They had never seen white children before. They pointed to Isaac's jacket and heavy shoes. When they saw Joseph's light, curly hair, they all began to laugh. I suppose they wondered how a boy could have hair like that, for Indians always have black hair and it is never curly.

After a supper of corn bread and fish, the boys were given a bed on a blanket in one of the wigwams.

When all was quiet, Joseph whispered softly, "Our fathers can never find us here. I am sure they cannot."

"No," answered Isaac, "I am afraid they can't. But we must not let the Indians know we are unhappy. We will stay near the camp and try to do just as they tell us. When they see that we do not try to run away, they will not watch us so closely. Sometime we shall be able to escape."

The next morning an Indian woman led Isaac and Joseph to a large stone bowl under a tree. She poured some corn into the bowl and showed them how to pound it with a stone mallet. This is the way the Indians make meal for their bread. It is very hard work, and it takes a long time to make a bowl of meal.

While the boys were pounding the corn, two of the Indian men took their bows and arrows and went into the forest to hunt. The others sat around the camp fire smoking and talking. They never offered to go into the field and help the women, who were stripping the ears of corn from the stalks and putting them in large baskets. When one of these great baskets was filled, a squaw knelt beside it, and, placing its strap of skin across her forehead, raised the heavy load to her back.

No Indian brave would work in the cornfield or carry a burden. "That work is for squaws and captives," they said.

"She showed them how to pound corn with a stone mallet"

As the Indians sat around the fire, some of them made snares and traps to catch game. When the corn in the bowl was all ground, one of the men called the boys to him and showed them how to make a whistle to call the wild turkeys.

Isaac took out his own sharp pocketknife to cut the reed. The Indians all wished to look at it; they opened its two large blades and tried them on a stick. When the knife came back to the Indian who was teaching the boys to make the whistle, he kept it and handed Isaac his clumsy, dull knife. You may be sure Joseph left his knife safe in his pocket after he had seen the fate of Isaac's.

Presently the two hunters came home, but they did not bring a deer. One of them carried a branch from which nearly all the leaves had been stripped. He called the women of his family, and, giving them a leaf from the branch, sent them to find and bring home the deer he had killed.

Scattered here and there on the ground they found leaves like the one they carried. Following this leaf trail, they at last found the dead deer.

When they had brought it home, they took off the skin and cut up the meat to be cooked or dried. A number of forked stakes were driven into the ground near their wigwam, and Joseph and Isaac helped the squaws to stretch the skin upon this frame, to dry.

In a few days the skin was hard and stiff, but the squaws knew how to make it soft and good for clothing. One brought a heavy stone mallet, and patiently, hour after hour, she rubbed the mallet to and fro over the skin.

Sometimes the boys worked upon the skin, too. They carried water from the spring and gathered brushwood for the fires. All fall they worked about the camp helping the squaws.

But it was not all work and no play for the little captives. The Indian children had many games, and Joseph and Isaac often played with them. They had races in running and jumping. They were very fond of a game called "ball in the grass."

The Indian boys made bows and arrows and practiced shooting at marks on the trees. In a short time they would let Joseph and Isaac play this game with them.

Many of the Indian men had guns, which they had bought from the white men. Sometimes they allowed the boys to shoot with these, for the Indians wanted the captives to learn to shoot well so they could hunt game for them.

The boys learned to make traps to catch deer, bears, rabbits, and other animals. They could make a fire by rubbing two dry sticks together. They could skin and dress game of all kinds.

When winter came with its cold and snow, the Indians did not go out to hunt very often. The deer were very hard to find. Many of the animals were fast asleep in their cozy winter homes. The ducks and other birds had gone from the frozen marshes. Sometimes the Indians cut holes in the ice and caught fish. Then what a feast they had!

In the winter the camp fires were made in the wigwams. The braves sat around the fire and made arrows. Some of the arrowheads were made of flint or of other stone. The Indians had no sharp tools with which to shape the arrowheads. They had to chip them into shape with another stone.

Sometimes the arrows were tipped with a sharp point of deer horn, or the spur of a wild turkey. The arrowheads were bound to a shaft of wood with cords of deerskin.

When the arrows were done, the Indian marked them so that he could always tell his own. If two Indians claimed to have killed the same deer, a glance at the arrow sticking in it settled the question. Indians often used the same arrow many times.

As the Indians sat around the fire making arrowheads, they told stories of the great deeds they had done. Sometimes they told the fanciful legends of their people.

The little Indian children listened to these stories, their black eyes round with wonder. Joseph and Isaac listened too, and the Indians would have been surprised to know how much they understood. They were bright boys, and after they had lived in the camp a few weeks they knew a good many Indian words. As time went on, they learned more and more of the language.

"We must not let the Indians know that we understand them so well, or we will never find out what they mean to do with us," said Isaac. So they pretended to be very stupid, and the Indians talked to them by signs, or in the few English words they knew.

The squaws, too, enjoyed the stories the braves told. While they listened their quick fingers worked upon a pair of deerskin leggings or other clothing. One of the women made Joseph a pair of soft deerskin moccasins and trimmed them with beads. She made the soles of thick, strong skin. She left a little of the hair on the skin to keep his feet from slipping. The moccasins were very warm and comfortable, and made no noise when Joseph walked.

In the wigwam where the boys lived was an old grandmother, wrinkled and bent with age. She no longer worked in the cornfields, or carried heavy burdens on her back when the Indians moved their camp.

Hanging from the walls of the wigwam were bunches of long grasses, and reeds, and the fine fibers of the cedar roots. Many of them had been colored red, brown, or yellow, with the juices of roots and berries.

Day after day the old woman sat on her mat before the fire, weaving these grasses into beautiful baskets. Some were coarse and large, made of reeds of one color. Others were very fine and had beautiful patterns woven into them.

In a large wigwam at one end of the village, the Indian men were building a canoe. They made the framework of strong cedar boughs, and drove stakes into the ground on each side of the frame to keep it in shape.

Near the lake grew a large birch tree. Its bark was smooth and white. The Indians cut the bark around the tree just below the branches, and again just above the ground. Then they cut it down the trunk from top to bottom, and carefully stripped the bark from the tree.

"Winter bark makes the best canoe," they said. "See how strong and thick it is!"

Then they carefully shaped the bark to cover the frames, and sewed the seams with the fibers of the larch tree. It took them many weeks to build the canoe. When it was done it would carry eight or ten people.

Isaac heard the Indians talking about a long journey they would take in their canoes when spring came. "In the Moon of Leaves the ice will be gone from the rivers and lakes. Then we go to visit our French brothers in Canada," they said.

"I know of two people in this camp who will never go to Canada," thought Isaac.

"Day after day the old woman sat on her mat . . . weaving . . baskets"

At last April came. The ice in the rivers broke up and slowly drifted away. The snow was gone, and on the sunny hillsides the grass was quite green. The birds came back from the southland, and the creatures that live in the forest awoke from their long winter nap.

Then one night, when the Indians thought their captives were asleep, Isaac heard them planning their journey. In a few days they would start to Canada to sell the boys to the French.

"We can find plenty of food in the forest now," they said. "The ice is out of the rivers. We will take our furs and the palefaces to the north."

All night long Isaac thought how they might escape. He knew the English settlements were far to the south. How could he and Joseph reach them with no one to guide? There were no paths through the forest.

He made up his mind to try it anyway. They would be guided by the stars at night, and the sun by day. Even if they died in the forest, it would be better than being sold to the French.

The next day the Indians went out hunting, and while they were gone Isaac told Joseph what he had heard. "I am going to run away tonight," he said. "When I waken you, do not make any noise. Just follow me."

When the Indians came home they brought two large deer. During the day Isaac hid a large piece of the meat and some bread in the bushes near the spring. He and Joseph also filled their pockets with parched corn.

That night Isaac was so excited that he could not sleep. The great camp fire burned lower and lower. At last all was quiet about the camp. He wondered if all were asleep. He could hear the heavy breathing of the two men in his wigwam.

Then he shook Joseph gently, but the boy was fast asleep and did not stir. He shook him again. "What is the matter?" said Joseph, in a loud voice.

In a moment Isaac's head was upon his blanket and he pretended to be fast asleep. He thought everyone in the camp must have heard Joseph, and expected they would all come running to the wigwam.

But the Indians, tired after their day's hunting, slept soundly. Again Isaac shook Joseph and said, in a whisper "Keep quiet! Come with me."

The two boys crept silently out of the wigwam, taking a gun with them.

When they were safe outside, they ran to the spring to get the meat and bread; then they hurried away through the forest. On they ran, over logs, and through streams, keeping always to the south.

When the first dim light of morning came, they began to look around for a place to hide during the day. They dared not build a fire to cook the meat, so they ate some of their bread and parched corn. Then they crept into a large hollow log to hide until dark.

"They will miss us in the morning, and will soon be on our trail," said Joseph. He was quite right.

"Hark!" said Joseph a few hours later. "I hear the barking of dogs! The Indians are coming!"

"Lie still and they may not find us," whispered Isaac.

The dogs came bounding through the forest, easily following the scent. They were far ahead of their masters. When they came to the hollow log they barked joyfully.

Joseph covered his face with his hands, in terror, but Isaac was more quick-witted. He said softly, "Good Bose! Good dog! Here is some breakfast for you." Then he threw the meat as far as he could.

When the Indians came up, the dogs were some distance from the log, tearing the meat into pieces and growling as they ate. So the Indians stopped to rest. One of them sat down on the very log where the boys were hiding. Joseph's heart beat so hard he was afraid the Indians would hear it. By and by they called their dogs and all passed down the hill out of sight.

All day the boys lay still in the log. When it was quite dark, they crept out and hurried on, guided by the stars. In the morning they found another hiding place.

Night after night they traveled. Day after day they lay hidden in a cave or hollow tree.

Now they were so far from the camp that they traveled in the daytime, and slept at night.

Once, just at nightfall, the boys thought they heard voices. They stood still in alarm and listened. Then they heard the barking of a dog. They crept forward among the bushes and listened again. Yes, they surely heard the murmur of voices.

A few steps more, and they saw the light of a camp fire. Around the fire sat a dozen Indians, smoking and cooking their supper. Joseph and Isaac were very frightened to find themselves so near another Indian camp. They slipped away quietly, and then ran with all their might.

When they were a safe distance from the camp, they sat down to rest. There was only a little bread left and only a few kernels of the parched corn. They ate what they had and went to sleep.

In the morning the boys were hungry and weary, "I hope we shall find a settler's cabin soon," said Joseph. "I am almost tired out."

"It is now six days since we left the Indian camp. We must be getting pretty near the settlements," said Isaac.

That morning they killed a pigeon. The smoke of a camp fire can be seen a long way. They were afraid to build a fire to cook the pigeon, so they ate it raw.

The next day they found a turtle. They broke the shell and ate the meat. They ate the tender leaf buds on the trees and bushes, and eagerly hunted for the roots that they knew were good for food.

Each day Joseph grew more weak and faint. On the eighth morning he lay white and still upon the ground. Isaac tried to cheer him, but Joseph only moaned and turned away his face.

An Indian woman carrying corn

"Come, Joseph, drink this water. Here are some groundnuts for you; eat these," said Isaac. But Joseph did not move.

Poor Isaac! What could he do? They were alone in the great forest, he did not know where. They were without food, and Joseph was too ill to go any farther. Still Isaac did not give up hope.

The brave boy lifted Joseph to the side of the brook, and bathed his face and hands in the cool water. Then he sadly left him alone, and with a heavy heart walked away.

Soon he came upon a clearing in the woods. Then a joyous sight met his eyes. A little cabin stood not far away. He quickly ran to it and knocked at the door, but no one came to open it. He looked in at the window. No one was there. He called loudly for help, but there was no answer.

A well-beaten path led away from the cabin. "It must lead to the fort," thought he. "Very likely the people are all there."

He ran back to Joseph, calling, "Joseph, wake up! Help is near!" He rubbed Joseph's hands and held water to his lips.

Joseph opened his eyes and tried to rise. Isaac lifted him up and led him a few steps. Then he took the fainting boy in his arms and carried him.

Isaac also was weak from hunger. His bare feet were sore, and his arms ached. Often he had to lay Joseph upon the grass and rest. Then he would take him in his arms again and stagger on.

Before night they came to a log fort on the bank of a river. The people at the fort were astonished when they saw the brave boy carrying his heavy burden. They were still more astonished when they heard his strange story.

The settlers from all around had come to the fort for safety. They tenderly cared for the boys, and, when they were well again, and the Indians had been driven far into the forest, these kind friends took them home to Haverhill. There all but the anxious parents had believed the boys to be dead.

Within an hour after they had been stolen, Mr. Bradley and a dozen other men, with their dogs, had gone hurrying through the forest in swift pursuit.

The dogs had led the way without any trouble until they came to the river. Here the Indians and their captives had waded a long way up the stream, and the dogs could not find the scent again. At last the search was given up, and the men went sadly home.

Whenever a boat or a canoe came down the river, a spyglass had been turned upon it in the hope that the boys might be returning.

Every stranger who came to the town had been eagerly questioned, but none had heard of them. Even Swift Arrow, the friendly Indian who lived in Haverhill, could not learn what had become of the little captives.

Until that glad April day when a boat from the fort came
down the river bearing the rescued children, not one word
had come to cheer the anxious friends.

The Candle

In the little village of Swansea lived a widow with her two children, Mary and Benjamin. The mother was a very good woman, always ready to nurse the sick, feed the hungry, or do anything she could to help those who needed her.

Indians lived in the forest around Swansea, and this good woman was always kind to them. When they were ill she went to see them, and made them broth, and gave them medicine. She tried to teach them about the Bible and the gospel of Jesus Christ.

Many of them came to her house, and she read the Bible to them. Nearly all of the Indians loved her and would do anything for her.

Among the Indians who came to this house was one named Warmsly. He was very fond of cider and would ask for it at every house.

When cider has stood for some time, we say it becomes "hard." Hard cider is not fit to drink. It is only fit to make vinegar. Warmsly liked the hard cider best.

One day he came to the house and asked Mary for hard cider.

"I cannot give it to you," she said. "It makes you drunk."

Then Warmsly grew angry and said, "You get cider, quick."

Mary called her mother, who said, "No, Warmsly, cider is wrong."

Then the Indian pretended to be sick and said he needed it for medicine.

"No, you can never get cider here," said Mary's mother again.

Oh, how angry Warmsly was then! His proud eyes flashed as he said, "You be sorry! Me pay you. Big fight soon! Indians kill all English. Me pay you! Ugh!"

Sure enough, the "big fight" came sooner than any one thought. The very next Sunday, as they were coming home from church, the Indians fell upon the people, killing many and burning their homes. This, you remember, was the beginning of King Philip's War.

But the Indians remembered the kind woman who had been their friend. They did not harm her family or her home.

But she did not forget the angry words of Warmsly. "I know quite well the other Indians will not harm us, but I am afraid of Warmsly," she would say. For a long time after this she would not allow Mary or Benjamin to go away from the house alone.

The summer passed and Warmsly did not come. At last Philip was dead and the dreadful war was ended. Autumn came, and with it, peace and thanksgiving.

"I think Warmsly must have been killed in the war," said the mother, at last.

One day, early in November, she began to make her winter's supply of candles. She hung two great kettles of tallow over the fire to melt.

"I think we will make a sparkler candle such as we used to have in England when I was a little girl," she told the children.

Mary clapped her hands in delight.

"I think there can be no harm in a sparkler candle," thought Benjamin's mother, as she sent him to find a goose quill.

When he came back, she showed him how to put a little powder into it. Very carefully the quill of powder was tied to a wick which hung over a small stick.

Then Mary and Benjamin held the stick and let the wick down into the melted tallow. When they drew it up, it was covered with the tallow. This soon grew hard, and they dipped it again. Now they could hardly see the quill or the wick because of the thick white coat of tallow around them. The candle grew thicker each time it was dipped, and at last it was done.

"Now you must not put it where it is too cold or it will crack," said their mother. So they put it up on the kitchen shelf where they could look at it.

"Oh, it is more than a month until the party," said the mother. "The candle will grow yellow and ugly if you leave it there."

So it was carefully wrapped in paper and put away in a box; but every few days the children would get it out and look at it. They would gently rub its smooth sides and wonder just where that quill of powder was hidden.

Would the day never come?   Weeks before, they had invited every child in the school to a special party, but since there were only ten pupils, it did not make a very large party after all.

Benjamin hunted for the rosiest apples and the sweetest nuts, and put them away for the candle party. From the beams above the fireplace hung many ears of pop corn, dry and shining.

At last the party day came. But no one thought of staying home from school or work because it was special. So the children all went to school, and it was well they did, for the day would have seemed endless to them. The party was in the evening, and the candle must not be lighted until dark.

But "dark" comes very early during the winter time, and as soon as the little folks were made clean and ready after school, it was time to go to the party.

In the big kitchen a fire burned merrily in the fireplace. How the flames snapped and crackled as they leaped up the great chimney!

Benjamin passed the rosy-cheeked apples, and the children put them in a row on the hearth to roast. On the bricks near the fire they placed a pile of chestnuts and covered them with hot ashes.

The powder candle was lighted and placed upon the table, and all the other candles were snuffed out.

By and by the chestnuts on the hearth began to burst their shells and pop out. At each loud pop the children would jump and look at the candle.

"When that candle goes off, you will not think it is a chestnut," laughed Benjamin. "It will make a noise like a gun."

Then the story-telling began. The children did not have story books in those days. All the stories they knew were those told them by parents and friends. These were usually true stories of the wild life in those early times.

"What a fuss Tige is making!" said Mary. "What do you suppose he is barking and growling at?"

"I hear voices outside," answered her mother. "Very likely some of the parents have come for their children. I will go out and quiet Tige and tell them he is tied."

When she stepped to the door she could hear voices near the old cider press. Surely those tall, dark figures were not those of her neighbors. When her eyes had grown more used to the darkness, she could see plainly the forms of three Indians, who now came toward the house.

She hurried into the house and locked the door. She had hardly reached the room where the children were when, with a loud crash, the Indians broke open the door and came in. Great was her terror when she saw that their leader was Warmsly. "Cider, now!" said Warmsly, as he sat down near the table.

What could the woman do? She must not give him the cider. There is nothing more terrible than a person who is drunk. "It must be getting late," she thought, "and the men will soon come for their children. If I can only get Warmsly's mind off the cider until then!"

She passed the Indians apples, and nuts, cold meat, and bread, and they ate greedily. But they did not forget the cider. "White squaw get cider, quick," said Warmsly, shaking his big tomahawk with an ugly look.

"Oh, if the neighbors would only come now!" thought the mother, as she went slowly to the cupboard. She took down a large brown pitcher and set it on the table. Then she slowly walked back to the cupboard and took down her pewter mugs, one at a time.

The Indians watched her with eager eyes. "White squaw get cider, quick," repeated Warmsly, looking uglier than ever.

But the words were hardly out of his mouth when there was a great flash of light. Puff! bang! went the candle with a noise like the firing of a cannon. Benjamin had put too much powder in the quill. There was a loud rattling of dishes and windows. The children screamed in terror. Even the fire was much scattered and dimmed with a shower of ashes. Then all was strangely still. The smelly powder smoke filled the room and everything was hidden in thick darkness.

When the smoke cleared away, the reviving light of the fire showed the hatchets of the Indians on the floor, and the kitchen door wide open. Not an Indian was to be seen. No doubt they thought the white men were upon them, so they made their way back to the forest as fast as possible.

That was the last the colonists ever saw of Warmsly.

The neighbors had heard the noise of the candle, and now came to take their children home from the party. How astonished they were to hear the story of the Indians! "God has been very good to us in saving thee and our children from the Indian warriors," they said.

Each year after that a special candle was burned in many homes, and the story of how one saved the children of Swansea never grew old. When the children who were at that party grew to be men and women, they told it to their children and grandchildren. And the grandchildren have passed the story down to us.

"Let us sit here . . . and watch for mother"

Two Brass Kettles

In a little town not far from Boston stood an old brick house. It did not look like a brick house, for it had been covered on the outside with boards.

It was the safest house in the village, and during King Philip's War the neighbors often used to come to this "fort-house," as it was called, for safety. When its great oak doors were bolted and its strong shutters fastened, there was little danger from Indians. They could not burn its brick walls as they did so many log cabins.

But no Indians had been seen for a long time, and the people began to think that Indian attacks were a thing of the past.

One Sunday morning, Mr. and Mrs. Minot, who lived in the old house, went to meeting, leaving their two little ones with Experience, the maid.

It was a very hot summer day and the windows in the big kitchen were wide open. The butterflies flitted to and fro in the bright sunshine, and the bees hummed drowsily in the vines twining about the window.

The two little children sat upon the floor while Experience built a fire in the brick oven and began to prepare dinner.

When this was finished, she drew her chair up beside the open window. "Now, little one," she said to the baby, as she picked her up, "let us sit here in the breeze and watch for Mother to come."

Experience sang softly and rocked to and fro, hoping the baby would go to sleep. But Baby had no thought of going to sleep. She laughed and crowed and tried to catch the pretty shadows as they danced over the window sill.

Suddenly Experience saw a sight which made her heart stand still. Behind a row of currant bushes was an Indian, creeping on his hands and knees toward the house.

Only a moment Experience sat still and stared at the Indian. Then she quickly bolted the door and closed the windows. There was no time to close the heavy shutter.

What should she do with the children? She looked around for a safe hiding place. On the floor stood the two great brass kettles which Experience had scoured the day before. She quickly raised one of the kettles and pushed the baby under it, then, before Baby's little brother could think what had happened, down came the other kettle over him.

Then Experience rushed to the oven for a shovel of hot coals. "If that Indian comes in here I'll give him a taste of these hot coals," said she. But suddenly she noticed that the Indian carried a gun.

"Oh!" she thought, "He can shoot much farther than I can possibly throw these coals." So she dropped the shovel upon the hearth and fled upstairs for the gun. "Keep still, children," she whispered, as she ran past them.

But the children did not keep still. They did not at all like being crowded under the kettles. They tried to push them over, but the kettles were too heavy. Then they began to yell, partly in terror, and partly in anger. The sound made the kettles ring with a strange, wild noise.

When the Indian appeared at the window, he looked around the room and could see no one, yet where could that dreadful noise come from? He stared at the kettles, wondering what creatures those could be that howled and rumbled so frightfully.

Just then the children began to creep toward the light, moving the kettles, which looked like two great turtles.

"Ugh! Ugh! Me shoot!" grunted the mystified Indian. Boom-oom-oom-m went the bullet, glancing from kettle to kettle.

The babies were frightened, but not at all hurt, so they howled all the louder and crept faster than ever toward the window.

Now it was the Indian's turn to be frightened. "Ugh! Gun no hurt him! Him come!" Then he dropped his gun and fled. He had no wish to fight with two great monsters that could not be hurt with a gun.

Experience saw him as he ran away through the garden, and fired at him, but he was soon out of sight. She could still hear the children crying under the brass kettles, so she knew they were not hurt. Before she could get down stairs, Mr. and Mrs. Minot came home from meeting. There lay the gun before the window, and the children were still under the kettles, howling madly and struggling to be free.

"What is the matter? What has happened?" the parents cried, and Experience told the story of the Indian.

"Perhaps he is still hiding somewhere on the farm," said Mr. Minot, seizing his gun.

He hurried across the garden, looking behind trees and bushes for the Indian. At last he found him, but the Indian could no longer do them any harm. The warrior was unarmed and filled with fear.

Comprehension Questions

1. Why was the "fort-house" safe?

2. What kind of day was it when Experience was watching the children?

3. Where did Experience put the children to hide them?

4. What did the Indian see when he looked in the window?

5. How did this story end for the children? For Experience? For the Indian?

Colonial Schools

In a very few years after the Pilgrims settled at Plymouth, there were many children in the colonies.

Of course these children went to school, but their school was not at all like ours. For the first few years there was not a schoolhouse in New England.

The children went to the home of one of the neighbors, who was teacher and housekeeper, too. They sat on a long seat by the fireplace and studied. When their lessons were learned, they stood in a row, with their toes on a crack in the floor, and recited.

The good woman went on with her spinning or weaving while they read aloud. The girls were taught to spin and sew, as well as to read and write. Each little girl took her box of sewing to school.

In those days nearly every little girl made a sampler of linen. On this sampler she worked in colored silks, all the letters of the alphabet and the numbers to ten. She worked her name, and age, and the date on it, too. Have you ever seen any of these quaint old samplers? It took a child a long, long time to work all the pretty stitches on one.

After a few years log schoolhouses were built, each having at one end a long chimney with a wide fireplace and oiled paper in the windows instead of glass. There were long benches made of logs split in two running almost across the room.

The largest boys and girls sat on the higher back seats, and the little ones sat in front near the teacher. All studied their lessons aloud, so the teacher might know they were doing it well.

"They stood in a row, with their toes on a crack"

The hum of their voices might be heard as far as the road. If you had been passing a school in those days, you would have thought there was a very large hive of bees buzzing near the school.

The little ones learned their lessons from a little book called *The New England Primer*. It did not have pretty pictures and interesting stories in it, as our primers have. There was an odd little picture for each letter of the alphabet, and beside it, a rhyme. The children also learned many verses from the Bible.

When a boy did not learn his lessons, he had to wear a tall paper cap called a "dunce cap," and stand on a stool in the corner.

There were wide cracks between the logs of the schoolhouse, and in the winter the room, except near the fire, was very cold.

The parents of each child had to send a load of wood to heat the schoolhouse. If they did not do this, their child had to sit shivering in the coldest part of the room. His little hands would be blue and numb with the cold, and his stiff little feet would ache.

This seems pretty hard, and I am sure the teacher must sometimes have brought the poor little fellow to a seat near the warm blaze. But they must have wood for the schoolhouse, and there was plenty of it in the forest near by; all the people had to do was to get it.

If a man would not take the trouble to cut the wood and bring it to the schoolhouse, his little ones must go cold. No father could stand that, so the wood was usually brought within a few days.

The parents of the children paid the teacher in corn, barley, and other things which they raised on their farms. Or, if the teacher were a man, the mothers sometimes wove cloth for his coat, or knitted stockings and mittens for him.

Comprehension Questions

1. Where did the children first go to school?

2. What did nearly every little girl make in those days?

3. Describe a log schoolhouse.

4. What did the children read from?

5. What did each family send to school and how were the teachers paid?

A colonial foot stove

Holy Days

For the Puritans the Sabbath began at sunset on Saturday, and no child could play after the sunset gun was heard. The evening was spent in reading the Bible and learning verses from it.

As Saturday evening approached, Hope ran to her bed to get her doll named Mary Ellen. Presently her mother came in and said, "This is the Sabbath now, Hope. You must not play with your doll on the Sabbath."

So Hope kissed her baby and carried it into the bedroom to find a safe warm place for it to stay until the next evening. There lay her father's Sunday coat; what cozier nest could she find for Mary Ellen than its big pocket?

Early Sunday morning, Mistress Brown came to the children's bed and awakened them. "Get up, little girls," she said. "This is the Lord's Day and we must not waste it in bed."

After breakfast the family had prayers, after which they did such work as must be done, and then dressed for meeting.

Master Brown filled the little tin foot stove with hot coals from the hearth. Then he took down his gun from its hook and looked to see that it was ready for use. In those days no man went anywhere without his gun, not even to church, for the Indians were likely to come at any time.

Rub-a-dub-dub! Rub-a-dub-dub!

Is that a call to arms? Are the Indians around? Oh, no, that is only the drummer calling the people to church.

There were no bells on the first meetinghouses in New England. Sometimes the firing of a gun was the call to worship. More often a big drum, beaten on the steps of the meetinghouse, told the people it was time to come together.

At the sound of the drum Master Brown and his wife, with Elizabeth, Hope, and Aunt Faith, started to church. From every house in the village came men, women, and children. They were always ready when the drum began to beat. It was not the custom to be late to meeting and as for staying away, one had to be very ill indeed to do that.

Elizabeth saw her dear friend, Mary, just ahead of her. Do you suppose she skipped along to speak to her, or walked to meeting by her side? No, indeed. "The Sabbath day is not the time for light talk," her mother told her.

When the meetinghouse was reached, Master Brown led his family to their pew. He opened a little door to let them in. The pew was much like a large box with seats around the sides. Each Puritan family had their own boxed pew with their name listed on the outside of the pew.

The church was very cold, for there was no fire; but the children warmed their toes and fingers by the strange little foot stove their father had brought from home.

They all sat together at one side of the church or on the pulpit stairs. When all the people were in their seats, the minister climbed the steps to his high pulpit.

*"From every house in the village came men,
women, and children"*

Only a very few people had hymn books. The minister read two lines of the hymn and they all sang them to some well-known tune. Then he read two more lines, and they sang them, and so on until they had sung all the verses.

Hope enjoyed singing the hymns. She stood up on the footstool at her father's side and sang with all her might.

Often there was another service in the afternoon. At sunset the Puritan Sabbath ended. Then the women brought out their knitting or spinning, or prepared for Monday's washing and the children were free to play until bedtime.

These Puritan families enjoyed real peace and liberty, for true Christian liberty is not the freedom to live as we please, but the power to live as God requires. Yea, happy is that people, whose God is the Lord.

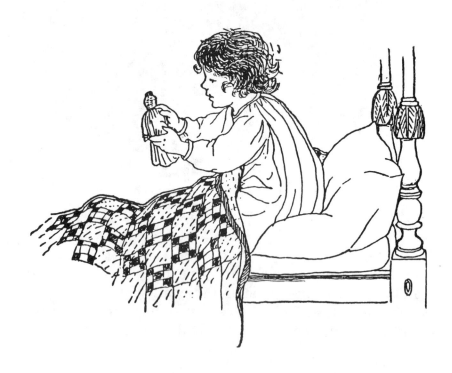